# An Intimate Charade

## YOLANDE KLEINN

Published by Yolande Kleinn, 2024

www.yolandekleinn.com

An Intimate Charade

By Yolande Kleinn

Cover Design: Aisha Akeju
Interior Design: Yolande Kleinn
Interior Font: Born from thehungryjpeg.com

Third Edition January 2024
Copyright 2019 by Yolande Kleinn

Print ISBN 978-1-946316-38-7
Digital ISBN 978-1-946316-07-3

*For Alistair & Alex. You know what you did.*

# Chapter One

The *Korria* made a particular sound when in transit. It had something to do with the engine manifolds, not that Addison Valdez was any kind of mechanic. The rumble was sleek and subtle, smooth enough that sometimes it faded from awareness entirely. Other times Addison could hear it anywhere, even at the end of the ship farthest from the engine room.

He found the low pitch soothing. It meant they were *going somewhere*, even if no sense of motion reached the interior of the little vessel.

'Morning' was relative on a cargo ship, even one so small. The tiny crew followed a regular schedule, usually chosen in deference to their last port of call. It allowed for their necessary routine, but it left the early morning hours eerily quiet. He didn't always like the quiet, but he savored the thrum of the engine seeping into his skin as he navigated the hall between the two largest cargo holds. Behind him, at the rear of the ship, slept the rest of the crew in private quarters.

Ahead he would find the only other person awake at this hour. The *Korria's* captain was chronically incapable of wasting any portion of the day, no matter how arbitrary the designation of time.

At the end of the corridor, the path stopped. Stairways that were little more than ladders led both up- and downward. Up into the cockpit, empty at this hour. Down into the guts of the navigation array. Between the two stairs stood a sturdy door, constructed of the same heavy material as the bulkhead.

Without asking permission to enter, Addison touched the panel beside the frame. He stepped across the threshold and into the room, letting the door slip silently shut behind him.

Galin Odona's office was an efficient space, inviting despite sparse furnishings. The walls stood bare and clean but for a single woven tapestry, bright greens in an angular design. A gift, Odona had told Addison once, from a sister who still lived on his home world. A tangible connection despite the distance of entire star systems.

Beside the tapestry, empty darkness hung beyond the sloping oval of the viewport. Despite the *Korria's* current trajectory, there was simply nothing to see. At quantum velocities the surrounding space would offer a shock of whites and reds. At rest there would be a perfect view of whatever planetary body held them in orbit. Here, traveling more slowly between sectors, the expanse of black was broken only by one or two stars so distant they didn't appear to move at all.

At the center of the small office sat a sturdy desk. And behind the desk, Captain Odona himself.

Dark eyes spared Addison only a glance before returning to the visual comm channel projected over the tidy surface of the desk. Odona offered no other greeting, but Addison didn't expect one. He was accustomed to waiting until whatever task he'd interrupted was complete. The fact that Odona didn't order him to leave was all the acknowledgment he needed.

None of Odona's other employees would barge into this office without express permission. Addison could remember the first time he'd done it, though years later he couldn't remember what he'd been upset about. Something that had riled him badly enough to override any sense of caution and decorum and send him storming into uncharted terrain. Odona had looked shocked as hell that first time, but miraculously unoffended. The stunt had inevitably been repeated, time and again, until it lost any element of surprise and began to feel normal. Just one more quirk of a strange but effective working relationship.

Today Addison found himself interrupting a long-range communiqué with someone he recognized but could not place. The face in the projected screen was Remian, a woman the same species as Odona. Her hair was trimmed severely short, a brown nearly the same shade as her skin, and large eyes conveyed an air of unflappable calm. Her face was attractive, guarded, and unremarkable.

"—wouldn't want to put you in an awkward situation," she continued without pause, either not realizing or not caring that someone had entered the room. "But I know I can trust your discretion. It's a lucrative contract."

From where he sat, Addison could see a perfect mirror of the image before Odona's eyes, but the woman on the other end of the comm line could not see *him*.

He didn't bother with any pretense of not watching his captain. Unheeded as he was, he could observe without detection as the conversation played out. Odona appeared completely at ease. Loose posture, relaxed shoulders, not *quite* slouching in his chair—Odona was not a man to slouch—he gave every sign of amiable nonchalance. He wasn't just crafting the illusion for an audience, either. Addison knew that posture too, knew just how much of a challenge his captain found it, and this was no such pretense.

"Lucrative and illegal," Odona answered with the faintest hint of a smile. Even his tone was relaxed.

"I know. Not my usual realm." The woman's face remained impassive. "But this is a family connection. My grandmother is anxious to find someone she can trust."

Odona's smile widened at the admission. His face, always striking, was distractingly so in the absence of his usual solemn demeanor. It was a handsome face, not remotely Human, though the difference lay only

4

in particular details. A heavy brow arched smooth and wide, uncommonly expressive. His ears were larger—a trait exaggerated by the smooth baldness of his head—and they sat low, almost exactly in line with the hinge of his jaw.

And of course there were his eyes. Unbroken black—the pupil indiscernible—with no whites at all. Addison had heard other species, other Humans especially, claim it was difficult to read Remian eyes. But he'd never seen the difficulty. Not among the *Korria's* small crew, all Remian besides himself, and certainly not where Galin Odona was concerned.

Unmistakable interest glinted in those dark eyes now. Whatever the proposition on the table, his captain was keen.

"It was kind of you to think of me, Karnis." Odona spoke the name with audible warmth and gratitude.

It took Addison another moment to conjure the rest of the name and match it to the face on the screen. Karnis Lor. Longtime acquaintance, occasional professional contact. She and Odona went way back—longer than Addison had even been alive in his shorter Human lifetime. No wonder Odona wasn't bothering to maintain his more professional demeanor.

"I can't guarantee anything," Lor said. "This might be a complicated prelude to wasting your time. I vouched for your crew, and she's anxious to meet you in person. But Anatoria Baell is... temperamental under the best circumstances, and this merchandise requires special care."

"Of course it does."

Addison sat straighter, eyebrows rising. He couldn't ask for details until Odona terminated the call, but his curiosity pinged. This wouldn't be the first time their little crew had handled illegal cargo, but they didn't make a habit of it. Not just because of the inherent risks, but because Odona's scruples prevented him from transporting the most common flavors of contraband. There were some lines one simply didn't cross, and Odona would sell his ship before compromising his principles.

He seemed ready to accept Karnis Lor's offer, which meant the merchandise must be safe. No weapons, no dangerous substances, no guilty conscience. But in that case, how lucrative could the contract truly be?

"I've made... arrangements," Lor said. "For you and Anatoria to meet."

Odona's brow rose. "Why do you say that like it means something else entirely?"

Lor's mouth twitched at one corner. "Because the arrangements are unorthodox. Discretion is obviously of the utmost importance. But given the lengthy vetting process, your presence requires an unremarkable explanation. A stranger staying on the estate will draw attention we don't need."

"So we'll be visiting under some pretext."

"You'll be invited to the extended lineal-kin reunion she's hosting, to celebrate her two-hundredth birthday. You will pose as a distant relative."

It shouldn't have been possible for Odona's brow to rise any higher, but somehow he managed the trick. "Surely your *actual family* will recognize the deception."

"Nearly three hundred guests attended her last reunion. Believe me, no one will question your credentials. Even I don't know half the attendees, and I'm coordinating the invitations."

"And what does this reunion entail?"

"Four nights." Lor's eyes cut downward to a sudden accompaniment of tinny beeps. "The entire guest list will be given accommodations on the estate. You'll need to socialize enough to provide a convincing cover. None of the events and activities are strictly mandatory, but..."

"But given the entire point of this pretext is to give your grandmother a chance to observe and evaluate us, we may as well consider our social calendar booked for the duration," Odona finished when Lor trailed off. Amusement softened an otherwise intent expression.

Addison grinned even though his captain was not looking in his direction. A crinkling of the smooth brow confirmed that Odona took notice.

"It will certainly be the strangest contract negotiation of my life to date," Odona observed wryly.

"I warned you it was unorthodox." Lor cocked her head just slightly to the side. "You can bring one member of your crew. Preferably someone who will make a favorable impression. Anatoria is not an easy woman to win over." Something cagey entered Lor's tone with that last comment. Addison heard it, and from the narrowing of Odona's eyes it was clear his captain had too.

"It's not like you to be cryptic, Karnis." Odona sat straighter.

"Not cryptic." There was no hint of nervousness or deception in Lor's tone. "Just trying to find a diplomatic way to put this. My grandmother is... particular. And old-fashioned. I've seen her refuse a high-volume manufacturing contract because she thought the company's name was an ill omen. I'm not saying you should lie about anything—*don't* lie, in fact. If she catches any hint of falsehood, she'll reject you on the spot. Just watch her closely and try not to linger on topics she seems to disapprove of."

Addison bit his lip to keep from snorting in amusement, both at the idea of an old woman whose business practices relied on superstition and a bad attitude, and at the thought of *Galin Odona* lying to *anyone*. Even the sort of evasive obfuscation Lor was suggesting would be a challenge for him. Odona possessed no talent for deception; it was another reason they stuck to shipping contracts that could be enforced in a court of law.

"You don't sound convinced I can succeed at this," Odona said.

"I *hope* you succeed. I told you there are no guarantees. She's already rejected everyone else's proffered candidates. I suspect she would deliver the merchandise herself if she could."

"We'll try to give her a viable alternative."

"Good. If *you* can't worm your way past my grandmother's trust issues, I don't know a single merchant who can."

The conversation tapered off after that, lingering over pleasantries and small talk. Lor promised to be in touch with more specific instructions. Then the screen projection vanished from the air above the desk, and Odona finally turned the full and intimidating weight of his attention directly on Addison.

There was no hint of irritation at being interrupted—after nearly seven years working for his stern and exacting captain, Addison was well attuned to signs of annoyance—and the glimmer behind those eyes might even have been affection.

"What do you think, Valdez?"

"Why are you asking me? Sounds like you and your friend already reached an agreement."

"I've agreed to meet Anatoria Baell. Even if she approves of us, we can refuse the contract." But there was also the unspoken fact that refusing would burn a profitable bridge. Better to go in with the intention of seeing this through or not accept the strange invitation at all.

Addison rose and rounded the desk, stopping at Odona's side. He hopped up to perch on the desk itself—he wasn't quite tall enough to manage a dramatic lean—and curled his fingers around the edge.

"Tell me more about this job."

Odona leaned back in his chair, tilting his head to meet Addison's eyes. "Smuggling medical supplies and equipment. Baell has acquired a large quantity of product, and she wants to move it from private facilities near Praxica to a pre-arranged buyer in Sector Seven-Four-Seven."

"That's a hell of a distance," Addison observed. "Not to mention it's Quadris territory."

Quadris wasn't just any intergalactic corporate conglomerate. Their government-subsidized monopoly made them a force to be reckoned with. Addison had never heard of them resorting to outright violence, but they maintained a reputation for financially eviscerating anyone who horned in on their profits.

No one could compete legitimately, which left the entire sector in an ugly position.

"Yes," Odona agreed. Just that one word. Inviting Addison to continue.

"There's also Anatoria Baell. She sounds... complicated."

"That may be an understatement," Odona agreed blandly. "But consider her position. No court will enforce the terms of a contract that violates shipping treaties, and the merchandise is enormously valuable. There are plenty of buyers who would pay double the asking price for this product. If she's going to hire us, she needs to be able to trust us completely."

"You realize if we're caught smuggling against Quadris interests we won't just be slapped with a fine or spend a couple weeks in lockup. You could lose your merchanting credentials for half a dozen sectors at once. You sure it's worth the risk?" As soon as the question left his mouth, Addison wished he could take it back.

In seconds the ease bled from Odona's posture, leaving him with the aspect of a man exhausted and wrung dry. Addison's heart clenched behind his ribs at the transformation. It was his job to ask the necessary questions, but he hated putting such a strained look on his captain's face.

"You've seen the same numbers I have. You know damn well we've barely scraped by the past few months." Odona watched him tiredly, and there was something almost conspiratorial in the quiet observation. Deception was not among Odona's strengths, but he'd avoided sharing the full scope of the *Korria's* difficulties with the rest of the crew.

Only Addison saw the full picture, and only because he'd wound himself inextricably into the administration of the *Korria's* business affairs.

"It's just a dry spell," he protested now, because the look on Odona's face made him want to *fix this*. "We've weathered worse."

"I can't ask my employees to work without pay." Odona closed his eyes, rubbing the bridge of his nose. "If we don't land this contract, I will soon run out of options."

"Sir." Addison desperately wanted to argue, but he didn't make a habit of lying to his captain. They'd endured lengthy lulls before, that much was certainly true. But he couldn't predict the future. For all he knew, this could be the stretch that finally flattened them.

Even if he could convince Odona to avoid this contract—which he wasn't particularly inclined to do—what alternatives could he offer? Odona wouldn't consider smuggling at all absent dire financial straits. If the *Korria* refused this deal and nothing else came along, they would be just as finished as if they accepted the contract and got caught. The path might wind a different direction, but the result would be the same.

They *wouldn't* get caught. Addison was confident they could manage just fine. They'd skirted the wrong side of the law a handful of times before and come out all right. But Odona paid him to argue. Addison could just as readily step into the other side of this debate, but that wasn't his role, and he braced himself for a final volley.

"You hate smuggling," he said more softly.

Odona chuckled, and the sound rumbled in his broad chest, steady and low. "Yes. I really do. Though smuggling medical supplies to people who need them? That isn't likely to weigh on my conscience."

Addison nodded. He knew Odona would just as soon keep to the legal side of the transport business, but there was room enough for the occasional exception. He knew also that there were lines Odona wouldn't cross. The *Korria's* cargo holds would never carry merchandise that hurt people. Never mind the heavy criminal consequences; Galin Odona would never cause anyone deliberate harm.

"Then I guess we're doing this," Addison said.

"I guess we are."

Addison hopped down from his perch. "I'm going with you to this reunion, right?"

Odona laughed harder at that, staring in mild but unmistakable disbelief. "I'm not sure that's a good idea. Karnis said to bring someone who makes a good impression."

"I make a *great* impression. I'm clever and charming."

"Yes," Odona agreed easily. "But cleverness is not an asset if you pick fights with everyone who expresses a differing opinion."

"You need me there." Addison glowered. "This is a contract negotiation. You always take me along for contract negotiations."

Odona just crinkled his brow eloquently.

Addison smoothed his hackles down with difficulty and managed to sound entirely reasonable when he said, "I promise to be diplomatic."

Odona considered him silently for a very long time. Long enough that Addison had to resist the urge to fidget.

"Very well." Odona sat straighter, shaking his head as though he still harbored doubts. "Rouse Keeth and tell her to lay in a new course. I've got work to do."

## Chapter Two

By the time they reached Falaris, Galin had done all he could to brace for four days and nights pretending to be someone he was not.

The fact that Anatoria Baell—the one person he truly needed to impress—would know the truth helped quiet the worst of his doubts. But even this wasn't a complete consolation. Galin would still spend the duration of the visit scrambling for half-truths and outright lies when speaking with anyone else at this ridiculous reunion.

He didn't relish the prospect.

His crew were little help. Laia Keeth was far too honest in her own right to offer viable advice. Edda Dak was too young to possess any relevant experience, for all his earnest desire to help. And Gamina Rielle had only laughed her most delighted laugh when Galin expressed discomfort with such a protracted period of falsehood.

Of course, there was also Addison Valdez. The only non-Remian among his small crew. Nearly as young as Edda, brash and candid and stubborn. For all the bluntness of the young Human's character, he had no problem omitting inconvenient information and adopting tenuous variations on the truth so long as it supported a worthy cause. The skill had come in handy more than once during the years since Valdez first boarded the *Korria*.

Valdez made it seem effortless, and maybe it was. His obsessive attention to detail was certainly an asset in keeping track of malleable fictions, a survival instinct that had proven useful plenty of times.

He had never used the skill on his crew mates. Seven years was ample time to learn a man's quirks and tells. Addison Valdez had *never* lied to him; Galin was sure of very little, but he was sure of this. The fact that Addison obfuscated so well when necessary was a practical tool at Galin's disposal, and the main reason he'd agreed to let Valdez accompany him to Baell's estate.

Galin climbed the shallow steps beside his office, stepping through when the door at the top slid automatically aside.

The cockpit was a cramped space—*efficient*, Keeth insisted—densely packed with equipment, but always tidy. A single massive pilot's seat took up the front of the narrow room, with a bewildering wall of consoles spread before and around it. Galin had long since made peace with the fact that he couldn't fly his own ship. In a crisis he could manage liftoff or a messy and perilous landing. But to truly manage these controls was a feat far beyond his abilities.

Laia Keeth turned her head for only a moment to acknowledge him. A smile softened round cheeks, and her skin looked unnaturally pale in the glare from the atmosphere. Her eyes were hidden behind protective goggles.

"Better hold onto something if you're going to loom, sir. I'm about to begin our descent."

Galin folded down the jump seat in the back corner of the cockpit and sat facing the main viewport. The tableau was stunning, the little moon that was Falaris impressive at close range. Only a corner of dark sky remained visible beyond it. The rest of the viewing field was taken up by a patchwork colony spread across the rapidly approaching surface. Massive domed structures stood interconnected, transparent building materials allowing a glimpse into cities and farmland and manufacturing facilities beneath.

The natural surface of the moon beyond the domes was a dusty blue, rough terrain that broke into gorges and hills, and even the occasional mountain.

Another moment—a gradual swell as Falaris expanded to fill the entire field of view—and then Keeth flipped a switch at the edge of her console. A red warning light popped on, accompanied by a shrill whoop of sound. The signal would be mirrored throughout the ship to let everyone know the *Korria* was about to drop.

With almost no atmosphere to disrupt their path, the ship descended smoothly. The cockpit rumbled, sturdy but reacting to the changing gravitational forces. The moon's surface rushed toward them, and one of the largest domes grew exponentially to fill the viewport.

Keeth had to raise her voice to ask, "You know Anatoria Baell owns the entire moon, right?" Her attention never left her controls.

"Yes." He *hadn't* realized that until Karnis's detailed information arrived. The invitation, the docking permissions, the directions for where and when and how. Tucked in with all that, he had found the salient detail he should probably have figured out on his own.

The knowledge had startled him then, and it still left him a little baffled. He'd realized from the first mention of this contract that Baell must be incomprehensibly rich. But to own an entire moon— not just the massive estate where she would be entertaining her extended family—that was a whole different order of magnitude.

He hoped like hell she opted to work with them. Galin and his little crew could use a patron like that.

With a final thump, more sensation than sound, the *Korria* set down beside the dome's smooth edge. They were just within reach of the connecting apparatus that would latch onto the side of the ship, allowing them to pass into the colony's pressurized atmosphere.

Now that the *Korria* was stationary, Galin stood and let his seat fold back into the wall. Through the viewport he could just make out a scurry of pressure-

18

suited dockworkers, securing the ship and maneuvering the airlock apparatus into place.

"Any plans for the duration of our stay?" he asked.

Keeth finished locking down the controls as she answered. "Sightseeing. As much as we can manage without traveling too far from the ship. Gamina's been researching, and apparently Falaris is one of the top romantic getaway spots in the sector."

"Is it?" Galin's brow rose. He hadn't known that when he assigned Keeth and Rielle to maintain the ship in his absence. Considering how little time off he was able to give his crew, he felt guilty for impeding their time in such a place.

"Yes." Keeth smiled as she tugged the goggles off her head and hung them on a hook alongside her console. "Don't look at me like that. We're here to *work.* You don't have to feel guilty about it."

"You also haven't had a vacation in over a year," Galin pointed out. For all the decades Keeth and Rielle had been married, he could count on one hand the number of times they had managed to sneak away together. Maybe he should reconsider, ask Dak to keep an eye on the ship instead. Edda Dak was barely more than a boy—had never been solely in charge of anything more arduous than stocking supplies—but surely he could handle the limited challenges of a docking port like this.

Keeth stood, stretching to loosen her tired limbs. "We'll have plenty of time to ourselves while you and

Addison are busy. I guarantee Edda will be off exploring the city every possible moment. And who knows, maybe after we deliver on this contract we can *all* take a break."

Galin smiled despite his own lingering doubts. "I have to *obtain* the contract first."

"You will," Keeth said. "Come on. The others will be waiting."

But only Edda Dak was in the common room when they reached the back of the ship. He sat on one of two matching sofa benches, fussing with a piece of fancy-looking luggage. Both sofas, bolted to the bulkheads as they were, had once been quality furnishings. Now they held more an aura of squashy disrepair—comfort of a different sort.

When Dak saw Keeth and Galin arrive, he finished sealing the travel case and rose to his feet. The case stacked tidily into a pile of luggage that perfectly matched it, the entire assortment ready for delivery to Anatoria Baell's estate. If Galin was meant to pass for a member of a family so rich the matriarch owned a moon, he couldn't very well carry his own luggage to Baell's front door.

"Where's Valdez?" Galin glanced toward the hall that led to the private crew quarters, including his own. He'd expected Valdez to be ready and impatient to depart the instant the *Korria* set down.

"Still dressing for the part, sir." Amusement sparked in Dak's eyes. "Don't tell him I said this, but he seems… out of his element. He was complaining the clothes are too tight."

Galin arched one eyebrow. "Are they?"

"No, sir. I know what I'm doing." Dak ran his fingers through a curly shock of hair. "I obtained exactly the right styles, in exactly the right sizes. He'll get used to it when he stops grumbling."

"Besides," Keeth added, donning the faintest suggestion of a smirk as she curled into a corner of the empty couch. "He only needs to survive four days. He's young and resilient, I'm sure he'll manage somehow."

"Just don't let him set fire to his wardrobe when we leave Falaris," Dak said. "These clothes were an expensive investment. If he refuses to keep them, we can probably get good resale value. He's small, but not so small I can't find *someone* to buy the set."

"I'll try and convince him they're worth keeping." Galin glanced down at his own attire—he'd changed before they began landing procedures—and found the clothes more than satisfactory. Not much different from what he usually wore. Dak had chosen dark colors and crisp lines, almost the cut of a military uniform. A little more restrictive, true enough, and he could certainly have done without the stiff edges of the collar-line that ended just beneath his jaw. The boots were more comfortable, black and smooth and made of an impractically soft material.

All-in-all, it was a look designed to impress. If Dak had done half as well outfitting Valdez, it might be to their advantage to keep the clothes and press the look into service occasionally.

"Engine's on cool-down and airlock procedures are complete," Gamina Rielle announced from the door. She slipped into the room, all grace and no flourish, and made straight for Keeth. Rielle still wore the gray coveralls she favored for working, and her dark skin shone faintly with sweat from the heat of the engine compartment. Black hair, frequently to be seen coiling in tight curls halfway down her back, had been intricately braided for the sake of safety. Loose hair was not an advantage when performing mechanical tasks, and landing the *Korria* was especially delicate work.

When Rielle dropped to the sofa, Keeth raised an arm to let her close. Rielle slouched into her wife's personal space and took her hand, brushing their fingers together in a gesture both intimate and possessive. It was a gesture that announced a fact everyone aboard the *Korria* already knew: *this woman is my mate.*

Married twenty years, mated even longer, Gamina Rielle and Laia Keeth still behaved with the same overwhelming affection as the day Galin had met them.

He was jealous sometimes, not that he would ever admit it. Not of either Keeth or Rielle, but of the attachment they shared. Remians tended to mate for life, but it was rare to see a pair so perfectly and devotedly matched.

"Do I really have to wear this?" Valdez's voice cut through the quiet room, measured but with a petulant note that made it difficult not to smile in answer.

Galin turned to assure him that, yes, the attire was entirely necessary—

But every intelligent syllable died on his tongue, leaving him gawping in silence as Valdez stormed through the door.

For a moment Galin's pulse thundered so loudly he feared his entire crew could hear, gathered as they were in close proximity. He stared wordlessly, caught off guard by the sight of Addison Valdez dressed in the same sleek formalwear he himself had adopted for the sake of this farce.

Valdez scowled as he stopped just inside the door, crossing his arms over his chest. His spine was straight, his shoulders tense, every feature projecting sullen disapproval.

The young Human was *always* pleasant to look at—more so than Galin ever intended to acknowledge—a constant distraction even in the weather-worn jacket and sturdy boots he usually favored. Loose layers were better for keeping warm in the lonely quiet of space, and for coping with unexpected circumstances in an unpredictable line of work.

But now, standing there in Remian finery of a more subtle order, Valdez was alarmingly, heart-stoppingly beautiful. Deep blue fabric with only the faintest variation in hue hugged the lines of his compact frame. Closely fitted pants tucked into soft boots much like the ones on Galin's feet, footwear shaped along slender calves and ending in an almost delicate heel. The shirt was a stiff material with a high-reaching collar. But unlike Galin's attire, Valdez's collar gapped open at the front, accenting the line of his throat. The dark fabric emphasized narrow shoulders, making him look even more petite than usual—an impressive feat when, as a Human of average size, Valdez was already the smallest member of the *Korria's* crew.

Straight black hair, usually tied back for convenience, had been let down to complete the look. This was Dak's influence, surely. Long, perfectly combed strands barely reached stiff shoulders, but the effect was soft and perfect.

Galin had been staring too long. Silent and startled. Guilty, because this frozen stillness was entirely inappropriate.

Valdez blinked, still scowling, and Galin saw that his eyelids had been smudged a deep, warm gray. The detail made his unusual eyes—all that white and the thin circle of brown around a black pupil—look even larger than usual. Galin wore a similar smudge of color, but he doubted the effect was half so striking on him.

He needed to speak. If his silence hadn't already struck the crew as strange, surely the staring would make Valdez uncomfortable. Any moment he would notice, and with his usual eloquent precision demand to know what was wrong.

"I told you I look ridiculous," Valdez snapped, jerking his attention from Galin to Edda Dak. "They're *too tight.*"

"They're not," Dak retorted without rancor. "They are perfectly sized. Believe me, you look so good you'll be fending off suitors."

*That* idea sent an unpleasant shiver the length of Galin's spine. But at least with Valdez focusing elsewhere he could breathe again. He could *think* again, and force the uninvited burst of desire back into the shadows where it belonged. He would not let this be a problem.

Four days. He only needed to guard his reactions for four days. He *would not* let any hint of impropriety sneak past his defenses. He had long practice making sure no one suspected his infatuation with a member of his crew.

The fact that these feelings centered on Addison Valdez made them all the more unconscionable. There was a visceral loyalty in the young man, a closeness between them that was not any sort of invitation. A trust that Galin strove always to deserve.

He had never given himself away before, and he did not intend to do so now.

Galin was a grown man. An *old* man he felt sometimes, especially beside a Human a quarter of his age. Valdez was only twenty-five. Not a child by any stretch—Edda Dak was even younger—but still so young the fact occasionally made Galin's head hurt. Humans were difficult to gauge, with their short lifespans, barely half that of the typical Remian. Galin had never quite known what to make of the strange and frenetic Human he'd inadvertently hired seven years ago.

Shaking himself from his distraction, he interrupted the conversation that had continued without him. "Let's move. Dak, go on ahead with the luggage. Keeth, Rielle, get the ship locked down for the duration, and start prepping for cargo just in case. Valdez, stop fussing. The clothes look fine."

\*

By the time he and Valdez reached the entrance of Anatoria Baell's massive estate, darkness had crept smoothly across the sky. There'd been no sunset. Between the lack of atmosphere outside the dome structure, and the fact that 'nighttime' was a result of the sun itself vanishing behind the enormous planet around which Falaris orbited, how could there be?

Plenty of artificial light saturated the main gate in the absence of the sun. Intricate lamps stood at regular intervals, glowing with a soft edge despite how brightly they lit their surroundings. Enormous windows on the manor itself spilled light across the stone path and staircase, sharp and tinted distinctly blue. Even the massive arch of the main door glimmered. There were twining patterns carved into the sloped frame, and among those shapes a thousand tiny pinpricks of light embedded in stone.

The stairs themselves were shallow but sweeping, with smooth ramps cut along the outermost edges. Blue runners were spaced in parallel rows along the stone, the fabric so new it shone.

Valdez had not once stopped talking during their entire journey across the city, but he fell silent beside Galin now. Awe softened his features as he took in the scope of the architecture before them. It was impressive to behold. The facade stood enormous and bright, tall windows stretching multiple stories high. Beyond it sprawled walls that stretched even taller and disappeared into the distance.

Galin had examined a map of the compound during their last day in transit. He knew the estate was practically a township in its own right.

The abstract knowledge did not lessen the impact of seeing it in person. The wealth behind these walls… It was ludicrous to consider. What could one person possibly do with that kind of money? With a *moon of her own*?

"Are you ready?" Galin asked in a low voice as he and Valdez mounted the final steps.

"As ever." Valdez threw him a cocky smirk, then fell quiet as a stiff attendant—skinny but even taller than Galin—approached them.

"Welcome, honored guests," the attendant said in a voice even tighter than his posture. With a minuscule gesture he called up an ethereal data screen, though Galin couldn't see where he wore the corresponding device. "Might I have your names?"

There were half a dozen greeters dressed similarly, in greens and grays pressed into perfect lines, and all of them were occupied with the steady tide of new arrivals. Galin forced a bland smile and gave his name. His real name. Karnis had made sure he would be included on the guest list, which meant no one would dare question his connections to the Baell family.

"This way." The attendant shut down his screen with a quick swipe of one hand through the air and turned to usher them indoors.

The main foyer spread out before them, as staggering and opulent as Galin had imagined from outside. Scattered blue lighting cast staircases and stonework in soft contrast. The reflection in the dark floor looked like a swirl of galaxy. The ceiling stretched so high Galin would have needed to tilt his head back to see just how far up it went; he resisted the curiosity. Beside him, Valdez exercised no such restraint.

"Fucking hell, have you ever seen anything like this?" Valdez muttered under his breath.

Galin didn't have a chance to answer before they reached the front of a greeting line he hadn't even realized they were moving through.

Between one blink and the next he was standing before a familiar face, albeit one he'd only ever seen via data screen and research.

Anatoria Baell was not a tall woman—at most she stood a couple inches taller than Valdez—but she had sturdy shoulders and a face that seemed sculpted for disapproval. Sharp cheekbones and a suggestion of jowls made her handsome face appear to be scowling even as she offered a pleasant greeting.

"Galin Odona?" Her voice was brusque and deeper than he'd anticipated.

"Yes. It's… good to see you again," he said, mindful of the surrounding crowd. A simple and harmless untruth, but it still hitched a little in his chest.

Baell's face didn't change in the slightest, but her eyes gave a particular glint—one that felt distinctly like censure. He couldn't fathom how he'd managed to earn her disfavor already. Less than a dozen words, and ten seconds of eye contact, should not have been enough to make an ill impression.

Baell tossed her head, and long hair slipped over her shoulder in a cascade of silver curls. "I hope you had a safe journey. I'm sure you traveled a long way."

She stood with attendants to either side of her, leaning her weight on a plain, reflective cane that was clearly not for show. Her bearing was steady, but Galin could see an empty chair against the wall not far behind her. The only such piece of furniture in the entire immense foyer, and clearly intended to give her a break as the receiving line extended into the night.

Beside him, Valdez was surely taking in all this and more, cataloging every detail from the useful to the utterly pointless. Silent, for once in a very rare while.

"Thank you for having us." Galin gave a small bow of his head, then gestured by way of introduction. "This is Addison Valdez."

"Welcome." Baell nodded in return, then took one hand off her cane to wave them away in a gesture of clear dismissal. "Go on. Enjoy the gala. I have other guests to greet."

Galin glanced behind him and saw that the incoming line wound all the way to the massive entrance doors, maybe even through them. No wonder she was in a hurry to be rid of him. These were her actual guests.

"I'm sure we'll speak at greater length soon," Baell said when he looked at her again.

"Of course," Galin agreed.

Then he set a hand to Valdez's arm—wordlessly conveying approval that Valdez had refrained from responding to their host's blunt discourtesy—and guided their steps deeper into the foyer. Putting Baell and her endless reception line behind them with relief. He dropped his hand as they reached a wide open doorframe into another room, some sort of grand hall, still impressive but without the spiraling staircases or the ceiling vaulted several stories too high to see.

"What the hell was her problem?" Valdez muttered, confirming Galin's suspicions about the brief exchange. "She's the one who wanted to meet *you*. She didn't have to invite us to this pretentious shit-show."

"Easy." Galin cast a downward glance that took in Valdez's face. He'd been trying *not* to look at his companion, for fear of distraction or making him uncomfortable. He found anger flashing in bright Human eyes, and he soothed, "Maybe she's not good with people."

Valdez snorted and shook his head. "Right. Not good with people, but she invited three hundred extended family members to her home just for kicks. If she's got a problem with you—or with *me* for that matter—she should say so and be done with it."

"Or," Galin countered smoothly, "if she's predisposed against us, we should be grateful for the opportunity to change her mind."

"In four days." Valdez sounded distinctly skeptical. "How are we supposed to change her mind if we don't know *why* she doesn't like you?"

"We'll figure something out. But right now, I need you calm. You're not going to make us any friends if you go into this looking for a fight." He was all too familiar with Valdez's temper, occasional but abrupt. He'd never seen it lead to a physical altercation, but there were plenty of ways besides fisticuffs for Valdez to get them in trouble at a function like this.

Thankfully, Valdez seemed to not just hear him but to *actually listen*. Those expressive eyes closed for just a moment, and he drew a slow breath. When he looked at Galin again, he wore a more placid air.

They both remained silent for a moment as Valdez's gaze began to roam, curious and restless. There was a lot to take in, especially for a young man who had spent his entire life in shipyards and space ports. Galin wondered what all this looked like from Valdez's perspective. Probably ridiculous. Galin certainly found the show of wealth excessive. In all his years courting business contracts, he'd never seen anything quite like this.

"Fine," Valdez said at last. "Now what?"

"Now we mingle and pretend we belong here." Galin turned his attention across the crowded room. Most of the guests were Remian—no surprise there since this was ostensibly a family reunion—but there were other species. Riss and Kayyey and D'Arveshe visible in glimpses. Even a handful of Humans besides Valdez himself, which meant hopefully the two of them attending together wouldn't draw suspicion among the largely uniform multitude.

Galin did his best not to speak to anyone as he led the way deeper into the sea of guests. His cover was thin, and he had never possessed a knack for superficial conversation. The challenge seemed even greater here, in this room where the most innocuous topics would require him to conjure fictions out of the air.

He hadn't told Valdez to stay close, but he was still startled to look around after only a short while and realize Valdez had disappeared. In his efforts to avoid paying undue attention, Galin had apparently overcompensated. Allowing Valdez to slip away entirely unnoticed, when normally Galin tried to keep a thorough and constant awareness of his own surroundings.

Valdez's unexpected absence presented no real difficulty. There was no reason they had to remain side-by-side through this surreal and far too social evening. Presumably Valdez had disappeared in order to listen and engage and try to glean information about their host. Considering Galin's own reticence— not to mention his lack of subtlety—it would likely be a feat more easily accomplished without him. And considering Valdez's earnest charm, Galin was confident he would manage the trick without giving them away.

Galin took one last glance around—no sign of Valdez within his line of sight—and went in search of a drink. Something cold and sweet, but not so potent as to muddle his head. A glass he could hide behind at the very least. A party this fancy was sure to serve only the best stores of spiced Remian ale.

He had a damn long night ahead. He might as well make the most of it.

# Chapter Three

Addison took his time exploring the noisy celebration. A dozen rooms interconnected to accommodate the crowd, each of them just as impressive and ridiculous as the last. Arched doorways had been propped open, wide and inviting between each vast room, and the number of people swelled higher every moment.

It was strange and not entirely pleasant to be surrounded by so many strangers. In Addison's work, during his time on Odona's ship, he'd grown accustomed to quiet. Calm. Personal space. For all the splendor this manor offered, the crush of people made it seem less like an expensive gathering and more like an over-crowded spaceport concourse.

He'd never felt quite this out of place in a spaceport, though.

He listened more than he talked, maneuvering between groups and trying—for once in his life—to remain inconspicuous. There was something almost cloying in the conversations, no matter the subject under discussion. Most of the pleasantries felt exaggerated and superficial, edging on strained discomfort. Addison found the entire affair baffling.

These people were supposed to be a *family*. Distant maybe, but still family who had traveled across sectors and solar systems to be together. Yet every interaction carried an undercurrent of formality and the distinct sense that both parties had something to prove.

He found a small scattering of Humans near the windows toward the back of one room. They weren't speaking Miri like the rest of the crowd, but whatever they were using instead wasn't any of the Earth-grown languages Addison might have recognized. There were plenty he *didn't* know, and plenty more from the farther colony worlds. Hell, it could be a language that had nothing to do with Earth at all.

He didn't interrupt to find out.

His intention was to blend into the background and unobtrusively glean whatever information he could, but he couldn't entirely avoid being drawn into conversations along the way. That was fine. He'd spent his whole life pre-*Korria* talking to condescending strangers, albeit never in a situation like this. He could bring those skills to bear here just as easily as contract negotiation and resource management. The fact that he'd separated himself from Odona's side made it more challenging; his captain would know how to hold himself and look completely natural in this crowd.

Galin Odona could probably be among the wealthiest assholes in this room if he were a man of fewer scruples. But then, if Odona *were* such a man, Addison wouldn't be here. He wouldn't have joined

Odona's crew in the first place. Even as young and impulsive as he'd been at the time—a headstrong teenager rather than a headstrong young man with better judgment—he would have let the *Korria* disappear from his life as quickly as it had arrived. He sure as hell wouldn't have stayed for seven years. He wouldn't have chosen to stick with his captain through thick and thin and everything else.

But Addison Valdez had worked enough seedy spaceports by then to recognize that a man of character was worth sticking close to.

Unsettling as his present surroundings might be, Addison could at least be sure Odona would have his back. This more than anything gave him permission, however unspoken, to nose around the crowded gathering. Combined with Addison's other defenses—stubborn charm and a lifetime of faking confidence he did not feel—he should have no trouble scouting the lay of the land.

There was one small and unexpected bright spot, as an hour turned into two and Addison continued his explorations. Edda had been right. Even though Addison still felt distinctly uncomfortable in the tight, precise lines of his clothing, the looks he received were appreciative rather than mocking. Warm glances took him in, mostly discreet, occasionally more brazen.

Addison acknowledged none of the attention; he wasn't looking to be propositioned tonight. But the obvious approval made him feel less out of place. More solid in his skin. More confident with each passing moment that no one would simply *look at him* and know he didn't belong here.

He wasn't quite shameless enough to walk up to strangers and ask for gossip about their stern and disapproving host. But in the end he did not have to; plenty of the clustered conversations were already about Anatoria Baell. She was, it seemed, both a force of nature and an irresistible topic of conversation. The unquestioned matriarch of the family, doggedly admired and utterly terrifying.

Most of what he overheard was nothing new: information he'd gleaned from research en route or impressions he'd formed from his own brief introduction. But there were useful snippets. Details about her personal life, her social habits, her biases. He hovered near the periphery of one discussion for several minutes, studiously pretending not to listen in on the small cluster of guests.

"You're not serious," said a gangly individual with a nasal voice. "Emri is her favorite nephew. She wouldn't just cut him out."

"She did." This from a rounder, taller woman with hair so black it looked nearly blue. "I reviewed the documents myself. He's out of the business as of last month."

"But *why?*"

The woman gave a careless shrug, belied by the glint of gossip in her distinctly Remian eyes. "Because he refused to take a mate. She said as much to my face. She asked, 'If family means so little to him, how can I trust him with my life's work?' And then she signed everything over to Emri's youngest sister."

"That's ridiculous," a new voice protested. "That's—That's the most backwards, old-fashioned nonsense I've ever heard."

"Of course it is," the source of the gossip agreed. "But do *you* want to volunteer for that argument? I certainly wouldn't. For one thing, no one changes Anatoria's mind. For another, anyone who tries will probably get the same treatment as poor Emri."

Addison moved away as the discussion shifted from useful insight to detailed theories about what 'poor Emri' would do now that he'd lost his corporate position.

He knew a little about Remian mated pairs. He lived on the same ship as Laia and Gamina, and he was close with them. They comprised a vital part of the tiny family he'd found for himself aboard the *Korria*. Which meant he knew the two women were a mated pair *and* married, a combination that did not always converge. Some mated couples never married. Some—though incredibly few—married couples never mated.

It was, as far as he could tell, a complicated interplay of personal connections and social alliances. As a Human on the periphery, he'd never delved too deeply into the nuance of it all. But certainly not all Remians took mates. Addison had never considered the absurd possibility that someone might object to Odona's decision to refrain.

It would explain the unspoken disapproval on Baell's face when she greeted them at the door.

He needed to find Odona. There might be nothing he could do, but Addison still needed to tell him. Considering the delicacy of their situation, the sooner Odona had all the information, the better.

As he began searching for his captain amid the increasingly noisy crowd, he realized what he hadn't taken conscious notice of before: nearly every adult Remian in this room *was* here with a mate. He knew well enough the signals to watch for, even among the pairs who weren't making any effort to broadcast their status. The particular brush of fingers, fleeting but deliberate. The more universal gestures—arms around waists, a hand at the nape of the neck, a pressing together of foreheads just before two men parted and moved in opposite directions. Handholding and light touches and the kinds of caresses shared by so many other species.

He had once asked Gamina and Laia why Remians didn't kiss.

It could've been an invasive question under different circumstances, but thankfully it hadn't been that night. All three of them drunk and sprawled across the worn couches in the ship's common room.

Their usual frank honesty softened into something more intimately candid. No, not three of them—four. Edda had been there too, half asleep with his head on Addison's knee.

Both women had laughed at Addison's question as though it were the most ridiculous thing in the world. And then Gamina had taken on a sly look and informed him that no, thank you, she and Laia would much rather use their mouths to make noise. Where was the fun in something that kept one *quiet* during sex?

Addison had tried to argue the point, that night and multiple times since, but he'd never managed to convince them.

Kissing wasn't some universal common denominator throughout the galaxy. Plenty of worlds and species didn't kiss. Just like plenty of them didn't laugh, or hold hands, or experience hiccups. A person could go mad trying to figure out the *why* of these things.

But here—now—back to their present situation, Addison realized this might very well be a problem. Among this crowd of mated and married couples, Odona would stand out in ways he simply could not afford to.

Worse, the man was so damn *honest.* If Baell cornered him and asked why he hadn't taken a mate at his age—just past one hundred according to his merchanting license, which Addison had always assumed was accurate—Odona wouldn't bother trying to conjure some excuse that might placate her. He would give a completely truthful answer. They could lose this contract before ever getting a foot in the door.

His search grew more determined as these thoughts overtook him. During the past couple hours, he'd remained peripherally aware of his captain. He noticed whenever their paths crossed near each other; there were few people Addison Valdez was more attuned to. But he hadn't seen Odona in twenty minutes. There were so many rooms, packed with so many people. It was difficult to keep track even of a man as tall as Galin Odona.

Instead of his intended target, Anatoria Baell was the next familiar face he spotted in the crowd. Addison drew closer to where she stood surrounded by a small but rapt cluster of guests. None of them took any notice of him as he eased into a nearby circle of conversation—just far enough away to remain inconspicuous—close enough to tune out the voices in front of him and eavesdrop behind instead.

Baell's words carried easily despite the low pitch of her voice. She presented a strange contradiction, a confessional tone that was clearly intended to be widely heard. "Well. Who am I to judge? But entrepreneurial successes or not, there must be *something* amiss with his character. To be unmated at his age... It's downright tragic."

Addison's skin prickled with affront, even though he couldn't be sure she was talking about Odona. Hell, it could just as easily be her own nephew; but some instinct told Addison that wasn't the case.

"I never would have guessed he's a member of the family," an audience member chimed in, cementing Addison's certainty. "I hired Captain Odona myself a couple years ago. He did good work. Delivered the merchandise well ahead of schedule. If I'd known he was one of ours, I'd have paid him a better rate."

In his peripheral vision Addison saw Baell wave the proclamation off with a careless flick of her wrist.

"You would have done no such thing. I've seen your 'family' pay scales. You bilk your own kin worse than any outside contractor."

The entire crowd laughed loud and hard—out of proportion to the jibe—taking almost a full minute to quiet down. When Addison risked a more direct look, he found almost no change in Baell's expression. There was a glint of self-satisfaction in her eyes, though. She tapped her cane once on the floor, and the last chuckles faded as if on cue.

"It's such a shame," came a reedy voice from the perimeter of the group. "I mean, to look at him... An attractive man in his prime, and successful enough. Surely *someone* would have him."

"I don't trust an unattached Remian of his station," Baell declared with cool finality. "There is always room for family."

"Are you *sure* he's unattached," asked a low alto tone. "Perhaps his mate simply couldn't come."

"Oh, I'm quite certain," Baell said. "Karnis's information is never wrong."

Fucking hell, this was ridiculous. Close-minded and presumptuous and wildly invasive, not to mention a stupid way to judge a person's entire character. Rich or not, what right did this woman have to dismiss Odona out of hand? It raised Addison's hackles and stirred fury in his chest.

He wouldn't convince any of Baell's circle of hangers-on to consider a different position. Even one-on-one, arguing at his best, he might not manage the trick. Here in front of Anatoria Baell herself? He'd have better luck convincing them there was a spaceport for sale on an adjacent moon. And he sure as hell wasn't going to convince Baell she was talking nonsense. Worse, he couldn't even obtain the satisfaction of telling them off and making a dramatic exit. The *Korria* desperately needed this contract. He couldn't do anything to jeopardize their already precarious chances.

When an entirely different impulse entered his head, the space between thinking and acting lasted half a second at most. He eased himself nearer the group. No one took notice, even as he moved close enough to interject.

The reedy voice offered a final volley. "I wonder *why* he's taken no mate. A man of Odona's status and

connections... Surely there's been ample opportunity."
A perfect opening. Addison schooled his expression
into something that more closely resembled light
confusion than anger.

"Are you talking about Galin?" he asked with the
perfect illusion of hapless sincerity. He turned to
make eye contact with the tall, brightly dressed
Remian who had spoken in that wispy voice. "I think
there's been some misunderstanding. I hope you don't
intend to play matchmaker."

All attention shifted instantly from Baell to
Addison, and he maintained his earnest demeanor. He
didn't look away from his mark until a different,
equally unfamiliar voice chimed in from the opposite
end of the circle.

"I'm sorry, but... Who are you?" The question,
blunt as it sounded, didn't seem intended to offend.
There was genuine confusion in the tone. Addison
had just interrupted a private discussion. Their
conversation was none of his business, except that
they were discussing his boss.

Addison gave a dismissive thought to diplomacy.
It occurred to him only fleetingly that he had
promised to do better if Odona brought him along.

Too late now.

In his peripheral vision he caught Baell watching
him with a single eyebrow raised. She didn't speak,
though it was clear she recognized him from their

introduction near the door. There was curiosity on her face but no hint of confusion.

Without hesitation, Addison looked the individual who had asked the question directly in the eye. "I'm Addison Valdez. Galin's mate."

"Is that so?" Baell's voice rang clear and sharp. Not disbelieving exactly—though when Addison turned he found a hint of skepticism in the all-through-black of her eyes—but curious and interested. Her demeanor shifted as she took him in with an appraising look. "But... and please don't take offense at this... you're so *young*."

Addison didn't miss her point: that Galin Odona was very much *not*.

He kept any hint of irritation from his face, even as he bristled internally at the implication that it should matter. He knew full well that Odona was somewhere past the hundred-year mark, which put him solidly in the realm of healthy middle age for a species that often lived two centuries. The disparity in their ages stood all the wider because Addison was not only young, but Human. If it weren't for Edda among them—even younger than him—it would be easy to feel like a child among Odona's little crew.

The pronounced age difference did strain the lie Addison had just told, but damn it, who was Baell to suggest he couldn't be Odona's mate? Addison was a grown man. Odona was gorgeous, strong, sturdy—he was *kind*—an absolute catch. They would make a damn good pair.

Regardless of the fact that Odona *wasn't* his mate: who was Baell to imply they didn't belong together?

He let a hint of genuine affront flash in his face but still answered in a polite tone. "Not so young I don't know a good thing when I see it."

Baell blinked at him, brows arching in what might have been surprise. Maybe she hadn't expected him to rise to the bait. Maybe she just wasn't accustomed to people pushing back. She certainly held the rest of this crowd in intimidated thrall.

Thankfully, instead of taking umbrage, she relaxed where she stood. Her posture eased, and her expression softened by the faintest degree. She still looked nothing like friendly, but there was a twitch at one corner of her mouth and a new glimmer in obsidian-dark eyes.

Whatever reply she intended to make, it was preempted by a member of the waitstaff appearing at her side and murmuring something in her ear. Baell listened blandly, then gave a curt nod of dismissal.

She turned to address her audience and said with exaggerated solemnity, "It seems I'm needed regarding an urgent question in the kitchens. If you'll excuse my departure..." She left abruptly, with a swish of her long skirt and a heavy tap of the cane in her hand.

Her audience dispersed almost instantly, and Addison let out a relieved breath.

His relief was short-lived. Alone once more amid the noisily meandering crowd, his brain finally caught up with the reckless and ridiculous thing his mouth had just done.

Fuck. He'd just *lied to Anatoria Baell.* On purpose. He and Odona were here at Baell's sufferance. They were here to impress upon her the notion that they would make honest and reliable business partners—that they were trustworthy—and he'd lied to her face without a thought.

If she believed him, he might well have improved their chances of landing the contract. But four days was plenty of time for things to go wrong. It was plenty of time for nagging inconsistencies to sneak in around the edges of Addison's story and make their host suspicious. With one careless exchange, he'd managed to take this negotiation from challenging to fraught. Difficult enough even if he were the only one who needed to maintain the fiction.

But there was also Odona to contend with. A man unaccustomed to lying, who was uncomfortable pretending to belong at this family gathering in the first place.

An edge of alarm spiked in Addison's chest as he realized just how completely he had failed to think this through. It wasn't the first time his mouth had run ahead of wiser instincts—and it probably wouldn't be the last—but the knowledge did nothing to remedy the mess he had just created. If Baell learned the truth now, the loss of this particular contract would be the least of their worries. Considering the business connections Baell must surely possess, discovery could poison the entire sector against working with Odona.

Addison needed to find his captain. He needed to warn him—admit his mistake—before Odona had a chance to contradict the story he'd just told. He hurried his pace, searching with increasing urgency. The massive galleries and banquet halls were overwhelming now that he had a purpose. His usually reliable sense of direction repeatedly failed him as one archway led into a massive room almost identical to the one before, over and over, and through them all he still had no idea where Odona actually was.

On the verge of digging his private comm link out from its discreet pocket—the device was small enough to hide even beneath the uncomfortably tight contours of his clothing—Addison finally spotted him near a wide expanse of windows.

Odona stood alone, surveying the enormous room without engaging.

Before Addison could cross the crowded floor, he saw Baell approaching Odona with a purposeful stride. She was closer than Addison, swooping in from a side door that must lead from the kitchens.

Addison cursed under his breath and scurried across the room to join them.

*Chapter Four*

Galin startled when Anatoria Baell appeared at his elbow. Engrossed as he was in silent observation, he hadn't noticed her approach.

"Enjoying the party?" A spark of amusement glittered in her eyes, but he couldn't tell if it was at his expense.

"You have a lovely estate," he said, sidestepping the question as smoothly as possible. Of course he wasn't enjoying the party. An expensive and over-wrought gala, packed full of more people than he usually interacted with in a year, all of whom had been misled as to his identity? He could think of few places he would *less* like to find himself.

From the twitch at one corner of her mouth, it was clear Baell read the true meaning beneath Galin's evasion. But at least he'd been diplomatic, and she didn't seem offended.

In fact she seemed... Not warmer, exactly. But somehow more receptive than she had been during their introduction in the main foyer. More willing to engage instead of barely tolerating his presence. He wondered at the change. The fact that he no longer stood at the front of an endless greeting line could account for the softer attitude. But his gut told him something more was going on here, and he needed to tread cautiously until he figured out what.

He didn't need to wait long. After a moment of watchful appraisal, Baell *smiled*—a sharp-edged and canny look—and said, "I just had an enlightening conversation. Karnis didn't tell me your Human companion is also your mate."

Galin's eyes widened and his voice lodged in his chest. Denial froze his tongue as he cast his mind over the past couple hours, trying to identify what element of his own behavior had given the wrong impression. He was always careful to keep his private feelings locked safely away. Valdez was far too clever for his own good, which meant Galin remained perpetually on his guard, preventing even the subtlest hint from sneaking through.

He had gone to great lengths to make sure no one suspected his interest, unprofessional and inappropriate as it was. The idea that someone in this crowd could have taken one look and seen through him was...

Terrifying.

He opened his mouth, determined to find his voice and explain—

And startled to further silence when Valdez slipped into his space, appearing as though from empty air. Galin had no idea where he might have come from. He'd been doing his best not to track Valdez's progress through crowded rooms.

Even more shocking than Valdez's abrupt presence was the fact that, after a barely measurable hesitation, he nudged at Galin's arm and tucked himself smoothly along his side. A moment later and he touched Galin's hand, an intimate brush of fingers across skin. It was impossible to mistake the gesture, no matter how little sense it made coming from Addison Valdez.

Galin blinked, staring straight down into earnest Human eyes.

Valdez smiled at him, wide and sheepish. "I'm sorry I vanished on you. This place is *too much*." He stopped touching Galin's hand in favor of slipping an arm around his waist. Pressing even tighter against him, a maddening presence.

A heartbeat longer was all it took for Galin's lingering confusion to crumble away, filled in an instant with vexed comprehension. With this new information, he required no especial genius to figure out where Baell's misconception might have come from.

Galin forced himself to return Valdez's smile, praying the expression looked natural. Fond. He couldn't afford to let disapproval show through, or any hint of the stern rebuke he intended to deliver the instant they were alone. He hesitated only a moment before reaching up to tuck a messy strand of hair behind Valdez's ear, then draped an arm across narrow shoulders.

Valdez's grin turned warmer instead of fading, and Galin felt an answering heat beneath his skin. Inconvenient and uninvited, but impossible to quash. A twist of guilt followed with predictable speed. He had no right to enjoy this unaccustomed proximity.

When he tore his attention away—a task more difficult than it had any right to be—he found Baell looking on with bald curiosity. He couldn't tell how far she was buying into this farce. Despite the glimmer that might have been approval, there was something else too. Something sharp and measuring as she watched them together.

Even if she did believe this nonsense, what then? Galin couldn't fathom Valdez's purpose. The entire reason they'd come was to prove themselves trustworthy; lying to Baell on the very first night of their visit was short-sighted at best, disastrous at worst.

Galin listened without speaking as Valdez exchanged paper-thin pleasantries with their host. He made sounds of agreement where appropriate, too distracted by his own discomfiture to actively participate in the conversation. He hoped Valdez was making a good impression for both of them.

"Enjoy the party, gentlemen," Baell said at last, an obvious prelude to withdrawing from their company. "We'll speak again soon." Then she turned, leaning heavily on her cane as she made her way across the room. She moved with purpose but no particular speed as she vanished into the crowd.

Galin didn't hesitate to turn on Valdez once she was out of sight. He'd been dodging conversations with strangers ever since arriving, and it was easy enough to avoid making eye contact with anyone as he set a hand to Valdez's arm and cut a path toward the room's periphery.

There was no true privacy to be had at this gala. He didn't dare test closed doors or veer off into side corridors where waitstaff were perpetually coming and going. Not on the very first night, and certainly not when Baell's suspicions must surely be piqued. He settled for dragging Valdez behind the dubious cover of a tall copse of potted plants, painfully aware that the greenery barely hid them from the room at large.

He crowded close so that even in the surrounding din he could speak quietly, keeping his expression as bland as possible.

"*Talk*," he ordered grimly.

At this range, Valdez had to tilt his head back in order to meet Galin's eyes. He wore defiance in the jut of his chin, but his tone was sheepish when he admitted, "I may have done something... ill-advised."

A hint of headache throbbed at the back of Galin's skull. "Did you, or did you not, tell Anatoria Baell that we're married?"

"Mated," Valdez clarified. "Not married. Honestly, why are you even asking me this? You already know the answer." Familiar challenge sparked beneath the words, and Galin bit his tongue in an effort to curb his temper. Valdez had always known just how to crack his composure and warm his blood.

Galin had long practice keeping his cool—keeping his distance—and still he required conscious effort to maintain a calm expression.

Valdez was *maddening*. Galin should never have brought him to this estate.

"Fine." He unclenched his jaw with difficulty. "I'll rephrase. *Why* did you tell her you're my mate?"

"Because she's fucking *horrible*," Valdez hissed. Unlike Galin's careful mask, there was no hiding the edge of anger in the wide whites of Human eyes. "I heard her talking shit about you. It was painfully clear she had no intention of working with us. And all because she's got some weird hangup about you not having a mate."

Galin's brow furrowed. "Why does it matter whether or not I have a mate?"

"I don't know." Valdez straightened his spine and glowered more fiercely. "But the way they were talking? She obviously thinks being unmated makes you deficient somehow, and that's such bullshit! I couldn't stand there and not *say something*."

"So your solution was to lie?" Galin didn't even try to keep the incredulous edge out of his voice. "To hand them exactly the story they wanted to hear and endanger our entire negotiation in the process?"

Valdez froze, and in an instant the fight bled out of him. His posture eased, his glower softened. Every hint of challenge melted away, leaving something startled in its wake. He blinked up at Galin with a look of guilt, of sheepishness at being called out.

Whether or not Valdez had considered the consequences of his actions, it was obvious he now understood exactly how far he'd erred. Valdez possessed a brilliant mind for business strategy, but he was not built for diplomacy. Or for patience. Galin should not have brought him along.

Too late for such regrets. Galin couldn't very well send him away now.

"I... really didn't think this through first," Valdez conceded. "But sir, what else could I have said?"

"You could have said *nothing.*" Exasperation raised Galin's voice to an indiscreet volume, and he quieted with difficulty. "Whatever aspersions they were casting, I'm sure I've heard worse." Baell was not the only member of his own species to imply there was something wrong with failing to take a mate. Solitude was not a path commonly chosen among Remians.

"She's a complete hypocrite," Valdez protested. "Arguing that you're not reliable because you're unattached? She doesn't have anyone hanging off *her* arm tonight."

"Keep your voice down," Galin hissed.

He risked a glance through branches and fronds, checking to make sure they hadn't drawn unwelcome attention. No one was paying them any mind. When he returned his focus to this private conversation, he found Valdez chewing on his lower lip in obvious frustration. Galin drew a steadying breath.

"She's a widow. She's not being inconsistent. Just close-minded." He shut his eyes for a moment, willing himself calm. No good would come of keeping Valdez on the defensive. It was clear they both understood how precarious a position they now occupied, and it wasn't as though Addison knew the true reasons this lie ignited panic in Galin's chest.

"But—"

"No." Galin opened his eyes. "I don't need you to defend me. And I certainly don't need you to lie for me."

The words hit their mark. Galin could tell from the flush that spread bright across Valdez's cheeks, and the way he dropped his gaze, all hint of rebellion winking out. A harsh inhale was all the sound between them for several seconds. Galin deliberately did not interrupt the impasse. He let the quiet linger, ignoring the instinctive urge to reassure Valdez that everything was fine.

Everything was not fine. They stood in a new and complicated mire of Valdez's making, and the potential consequences were substantial. Valdez, of all people, knew how badly the *Korria* needed this contract.

"I'm sorry," Valdez said, soft and sincere. His chin tucked low, and he stared at Galin's chest as he spoke.

"There's nothing to be done for it now." The words were not an absolution, but Galin gentled his voice. He'd made his point; there was no reason to torture Valdez when he clearly understood the gravity of his misstep. "The entire purpose of our presence is for Baell to evaluate us. We're here to *prove ourselves trustworthy.* If we confess that we've already lied to her, she's certain to refuse us the contract."

"*Fuck.*" Valdez blinked hard and his face flushed brighter.

"We will have to maintain this charade of yours," Galin concluded, pained tension undercutting every word. His tone earned a flinch from Valdez, but Galin did not shy from his assertion now that he'd spoken the words aloud. "There is no path forward but through."

Another lengthy silence lingered as Valdez visibly bolstered himself. Straightened his spine, leveled his shoulders, raised his head to meet Galin's eyes with a glitter of renewed challenge.

Valdez's expression held warm and stubborn as he declared, "It's only four days. We can do this, sir."

Galin nodded, and prayed he was right.

## Chapter Five

It seemed an eternity before the crowd of guests began to thin. Addison stayed at Odona's side as one hour turned into two, night closing in late and heavy over the gathering. His captain, even quieter than usual, let Addison do most of the talking as they engaged with the dwindling crowd.

Addison made an effort to keep their conversations superficial. They needed this crowd to like them—they were here to make a favorable impression—but it wouldn't do to be too memorable. Little as Addison enjoyed this particular exercise, it was the least he could do after the mess he'd made.

Warm air tickled the side of his face when Odona leaned close to murmur, "I'm going to ask the waitstaff about being shown to our accommodations." The hand at the small of Addison's back disappeared. A moment later and so did Odona, vanishing somewhere behind him and leaving Addison to offer an apologetic smile to the small cluster of guests that had converged around them.

The vast room felt instantly chilly without Odona along his side.

He managed not to startle when Odona returned a few minutes later, slipping back into place as though casual intimacy were perfectly normal between them.

Strange really, how it *did* feel... Not normal exactly, but pleasant. Surreal. There was something solid in the weight of Odona's arm around his waist, tucking him close.

Odona's other hand reached to brush fingertips across Addison's knuckles, a subtle but deliberate gesture for their audience. "If you'll pardon our departure," Odona spoke into a momentary lull, addressing the entire circle this time. "It's getting late, and we began our morning far too early."

The words sounded easy and amiable. They gave no hint whatsoever of the truth Addison recognized beneath: that Odona was desperate to make his escape, to drop the act and the small talk, to remove himself from the still far too sizable crowd of strangers. Addison could certainly sympathize. He didn't enjoy the self-important company of Anatoria Baell's family either.

"Goodnight," he added as Odona steered him away, one last parting volley over his shoulder. "Maybe we'll see you all at breakfast."

They didn't wait for a response though. Addison sure as hell didn't care if he saw any of these people in the morning, and he couldn't imagine Odona gave a damn either.

A stiff-backed young Remian with ashy skin and broad shoulders escorted them from the main foyer, down a long hallway and onto a balcony. The balcony was expansive, its curved perimeter surrounded by open space. An expanse of grass and gravel paths spread out far below.

"Your assigned room is across the compound in Ruke Hall," their guide announced with prim gravity. The information was directed at Odona and Addison both. There was no hint of reaction in the shining black of those eyes, but Addison stayed leaning against Odona anyway. If they intended to maintain their pretense for the other guests, surely it was even more vital to do the same in front of Baell's paid staff.

Before he could ask how they were supposed to get across the compound, a small craft eased forward from the shadows beside the balcony. It hovered beside a break in the stone railing, perfectly motionless. The sleek side opened as a dark metal panel slid away, revealing a passenger compartment easily large enough for half a dozen occupants. Plush and smooth and somehow inviting despite being only dimly lit.

Their guide gestured them inside, then followed and took one of the remaining seats just as the side panel slid back into place.

At least the journey was quick. And in Ruke Hall, when their guide ushered them through an ornate door—identical to the others in the crisply carpeted hallway—Addison held his breath until the door closed and he and Odona were truly alone.

The speed with which Odona stopped touching him would have been a little insulting under other circumstances. But Addison didn't take it personally as he watched his captain poke curiously about the sitting room and then disappear through the only other door.

Addison took a moment himself to nose around, taking in the circle of furniture that filled the compact space—a couple of narrow settees and a tiny table beneath diffuse lighting with no discernible source—and the wide window running almost the entire length of one wall. There wasn't much to see outside at this hour. Just sprawling darkness broken by the occasional glimmer of artificial light.

Odona hadn't returned, so Addison followed his footsteps through the still-open door. A sliding pane, lightweight and opaque, it had been pushed aside and left ajar. Odona stood just inside, arms crossed tightly over his broad chest, his posture tense. A storm of disapproval thundered over his normally smooth brow. His all-black eyes narrowed and his mouth pressed thin.

"What's wrong?" Addison cast a look across the room, following the glower all the way to—

Oh. That wasn't ideal.

"There is only one bed," Odona announced unnecessarily. If his expression had not been enough to convey his displeasure, the offended tone of voice would have gotten the point across just as surely. Addison tried not to feel insulted.

"We could ask for a second room."

"They think you are my mate," Odona answered tightly. He was still staring at the bed, still standing with his arms crossed firmly over his chest. "That's why there is *only one bed*. We can't ask for a second room. How would it look after the show we put on tonight?"

"Right." Addison's shoulders slumped a little. "Um."

The bed was huge. Decked in blue sheets, it took up a truly ludicrous portion of the small suite, leaving only a narrow patch of floor in front of a sturdy wardrobe. Their luggage sat wedged in the corner waiting for them, and another door stood ajar in the opposite corner, a glimpse of a washroom beyond.

They could easily both sleep in the bed. They could share and not come anywhere near touching each other.

Before Addison could say so—and he was going to, despite the forbidding look on his captain's face—Odona shook his head hard as though dispelling an unwelcome thought.

"I'll sleep on the floor."

"*What?*" Addison gawped. Not just at the implication that they couldn't share a bed this size, but at the fact that his captain was volunteering to take the floor.

"It wouldn't be appropriate for us to share." Odona moved farther into the room, tugging open one of the wardrobe doors. Probably looking for extra bedding in order to follow through on this ridiculous notion of his.

"Then you should take the bed, and *I* should sleep somewhere else," Addison protested. "It's my fault they put us in the same suite. If I'd kept my mouth shut—"

"Valdez, it's fine. I've slept on plenty of floors."

"Yeah, but you shouldn't have to sleep on this one. I'll... I can sleep in the other room. There's other furniture." Awful, stiff-looking furniture that would probably be hell to sleep on, but surely it would be better than the floor.

Little as Addison relished the idea, he let the offer linger. He honestly couldn't imagine Odona would make him sleep in the other room. Appropriate or not, this didn't have to be a big deal. Living aboard the *Korria* meant sharing plenty of close quarters, albeit not this close. They lived practically in each other's pockets aboard ship. Why should their present circumstances present any additional discomfort?

Odona paused in his search for extra blankets. He kept one hand on the bureau door as he turned and caught Addison in an indecipherable stare. It was strange to look Odona in the face and not know what he was thinking. Addison had learned to read his captain well over the years. Even the others—Gamina, Laia, Edda—he'd never grown quite so attuned to. Never spent so much time and energy memorizing their every tell the way he'd studied Odona.

To look at him now and have no idea what was going on in his head... It was damned unsettling, and Addison didn't like it one bit.

"This is ridiculous," he blurted into the silence. "Of course we can just share the damn bed. Sir, look at that thing. It's bigger than the *Korria's* galley." Admittedly, the galley was not a large room. But his point stood. There was no logical reason they couldn't both sleep in the massive blue bed.

But instead of conceding the point, Odona turned to their luggage and hoisted one of his bags onto the mattress.

Addison waited, confused and uncertain.

"No," Odona said without looking at him. "It's fine. You've convinced me. You take the other room. If it's terrible we can trade tomorrow. I've slept on floors harder than this."

Addison stared, disbelieving as the proclamation sank in. He didn't protest—he'd made the offer in earnest and he wasn't going to argue now that Odona had agreed—but he wanted to. He wanted to ask what the hell the problem was. It stung, more than it probably should have, to realize just how horrified Odona was at the idea of Addison encroaching on his personal space. He didn't know what the hell to make of it, let alone how to respond.

"Yeah," he managed at last, voice mostly normal. "Okay. I'm sure it'll be fine."

*

It wasn't fine.

Sleeping on one of the tiny settees in the main room was every bit as terrible as his instincts had predicted. The seat was barely long enough to accommodate his height, and the narrow cushions and stiff back made it impossible to lie any way but sideways. He could feel the hours creeping past, broken only sporadically by a sliver of dream before uncomfortable consciousness reached him again.

If he were a little less prideful, he might have relocated to the floor.

Improbably, he nodded off just before morning. Long enough and deep enough that he startled into daylight, jerking awake at the sensation of a firm hand shaking his shoulder.

He sat up slowly, blinking sleep from bleary eyes. Odona was already dressed. He looked bright and well-rested and irritatingly handsome in a fresh ensemble nearly identical to yesterday's.

Addison forced himself not to glower. His eyes felt gritty and his back hurt. The thought of putting on a pleasant face and interacting with nosy strangers made him seriously consider arson as an alternative career path.

"How did you sleep?" Odona sat on the other settee, holding a steaming mug between his hands. It took Addison a moment to realize there was a second mug on the table beside him.

"Great," he lied. "This thing's not so bad."

Odona raised a single skeptical eyebrow and sipped his drink.

Addison kicked aside his blankets and put both feet on the floor, reaching for his own mug and praying it contained some form of caffeine. He knew Remians metabolized caffeine—the *Korria* had kept a ready supply of Terran coffee since Addison first introduced it to the crew—but that didn't mean Baell's estate was equipped to provide such specific luxuries.

The warm drink was delicious. Smooth and sweet without being cloying. And since his body instinctively perked up as though at a first sip of coffee, he wasn't going to complain.

"There's an invitation to breakfast on the guest comm," Odona explained. Matter of fact, as though Addison had actually asked aloud why the hell they were both conscious. "And then some sort of guided tour of the estate grounds and the city. All voluntary of course."

"Meaning mandatory for business contacts pretending to be guests," Addison muttered. He took a longer, slower sip of his drink. Whether or not it contained caffeine, his head was clearing by the minute.

"Yes." Odona set his mug down and rose to his feet, moving for the wall of unbroken window.

From where he sat, Addison could see daylight illuminating an impressive sprawl of greenery, interspersed with sturdy but sleek-edged buildings. There was symmetry to the vista. Despite the abundance of plant life, it was obvious at a glance that everything about these grounds had been constructed to exacting detail. This was life imposed on the uninviting surface of Falaris. Beautiful. But not truly natural.

Perhaps in a better frame of mind, he could have appreciated the structured elegance before him. But the bright sunlight hurt his eyes and made his head throb.

"Ugh." He drained the rest of his mug in a slow swallow and set it back down on the table.

"The washroom is yours," Odona said. "I'll call for transport as soon as you're ready to depart."

Addison rubbed at his face with both hands. God, his whole body ached. He couldn't do this. It was stupid and selfish and careless to refuse under the circumstances, but he couldn't face the itinerary ahead of them.

"No," he said.

Odona turned from the window and blinked at him. "I'm sorry?"

"No," Addison repeated. He kept his expression bland as he raised his eyes. "You can call for transport and go without me. I'm not attending breakfast. Or the city tour. I need to return to the ship."

"You need— Why?"

*Because you made me sleep on the fucking couch*, Addison very carefully did not say. "Because I left a cost-comparison report unfinished." It wasn't even a plausible pretext. He couldn't be bothered to conjure something more convincing. From the way both of Odona's eyebrows rose, his lack of effort hadn't gone unnoticed.

"You can't leave," Odona said quietly. Every syllable was measured in a way that didn't quite sound like anger, but Addison couldn't account for it any other way. "If you expect me to spend the next four days alone with these people, we may as well concede right now that we're no longer invested in winning this contract."

"Not all four days. Only a few hours. I just... I need a few hours, and then I'll be back." He needed space— his *own space* aboard the *Korria*—and maybe a goddamn nap. He could usually function on minimal sleep, but he wouldn't charm anyone like this. He wasn't an asset to the mission. He would burn every bridge at this gathering if he showed his face right now.

Odona stared at him for a long, uncomfortable moment before turning aside with a clipped, "Do what you want. But don't take too long."

Before Addison could answer, Odona was gone. Vanished through the door and into the hallway without actually summoning transport to take him to the main hall. There were probably other guest comms scattered through Ruke's public areas—in a place like this there would be no shortage of ways to contact the staff—but the speed with which Addison found himself alone was still jarring.

He couldn't blame Odona for being frustrated with him. Hell, Addison would be just as pissy in his place. Abandoned to this crowd with no warning, left with no choice but to hold the line without backup. It wasn't a kind position to leave anyone in. If Addison were feeling a little less exhausted—a little less helplessly selfish—he wouldn't consider shirking his responsibilities like this.

Addison called for transport of his own before finally departing the room.

*

The city beyond Baell's estate looked much the same by daylight.

Addison's ride—a passenger craft nearly identical to the one from last night—deposited him at the edge of the city's primary port. Addison exacted a promise that the driver would return in four hours, local time. That would be enough to get some rest, and to steady himself before plunging back into the taxing social scene at Anatoria Baell's estate.

Back on the *Korria*, he sat on one of the worn couches in the common room. Just for a moment. Just to *breathe* for a second.

He didn't intend to lie down, but he must have done so. He had no other explanation for the way he blinked abruptly awake—with no recollection of falling asleep—but feeling distinctly more like a person than a gravel pit. His whole body stretched lengthwise along the couch, with his head resting on one soft arm and his ankles kicked out over the other. The lights, which had come on automatically when he entered the common room, had blessedly dimmed.

More importantly, he smelled coffee. Real, actual, *Terran coffee*. Close at hand. He turned his head and discovered Edda Dak standing beside him, amusement in the quirk of his mouth.

Addison didn't even care that the amusement was obviously at his expense. He was too busy sitting up and gratefully accepting the steaming cup from Edda's hands.

"Didn't they let you sleep at that fancy party?" Edda's curls bounced a little as he tilted his head to one side.

"Mmm." Addison took a slow sip, savoring the familiar flavors. There was too much sugar since Edda had prepared it, but hell, he could deal with sugar. Between the nap and the coffee hitting his system, he could actually tolerate the thought of returning to Baell's estate and doing his damn job.

Maybe he would even apologize to Odona for his behavior this morning.

He wouldn't bother apologizing again for the tangle he'd created the evening before. As far as Addison was concerned, sleeping on last night's torture device was all the penance he owed. If Odona was still angry—and he very well might be—they would just have to find some other way to make peace. Addison sure as hell wasn't sleeping on the settee again.

Addison closed his eyes and zoned out as he savored his coffee. When he opened them he realized Gamina and Laia were both sitting at the small table in the corner. Drinking from their own steaming mugs and watching him with curious expressions. They held hands atop the table, fingers tracing idle patterns over wrists and palms. Not restless. Just intimate, subtle, familiar habit. Genuine closeness, so comfortable compared to Addison's own cumbersome attempts to emulate the same aspect at Odona's side last night.

"Um. Good morning." He was reasonably sure it was still morning. His returning ride would have comm'd to wake him if nothing else.

"I'll see you guys later tonight," Edda called as he crossed the common room, moving from the galley door to the short hall and the airlock beyond. The words were obviously intended for Laia and Gamina, though Edda spared a quick wave for Addison before disappearing.

"Where is he going?" Addison blinked after him a moment, then turned once more to Laia and Gamina.

"He's got a cousin working one of the entertainment clubs across town."

"Oh." Addison felt like a bit of an asshole for not knowing that.

"Addison, don't take this the wrong way," Gamina said with just a hint of wry humor, "but what in the name of heaven are you doing here? Aren't you supposed to be eating fancy food and drinking expensive alcohol on an eccentric's private estate?" She sipped from her mug and somehow made it look like a pointed gesture.

Now, rested and rational, Addison felt distinctly foolish for running away.

Hell, he hadn't just run away. He'd pitched a fit and stormed from the grounds, like a teenager throwing a tantrum. His irritation over sleeping arrangements seemed abruptly ridiculous. All the worse for the disproportionate cruelty of leaving Odona to face an entire estate of prickly company alone.

Addison wasn't *worried* for Odona. He would do just fine in that crowd—certainly better than he would've managed with a sleepless and short-tempered employee on his arm—but he felt guilty for leaving Odona to conjure excuses on Addison's behalf.

For not having his back after complicating their situation unforgivably.

For making his captain lie, when Addison knew full well the man had no talent for it.

God, how could Odona be anything besides furious with him?

"Addison." Laia's softer voice cut through the quiet, equal parts chiding and worried. "What's wrong?"

He took another sip of too-sweet coffee. The drink was already cooling noticeably in his hands. As stalling tactics went, it wasn't a very good one. It bought him a couple seconds at most. He could refuse to answer, but what would be the point?

"I may have done something stupid." He muttered the confession as though to his drink instead of his audience, low and sheepish, glaring at his mug. "And... And I think the captain's angry at me. But there's no way to fix it now."

"How stupid are we talking?" Gamina asked.

"*Cosmically* stupid." Addison forced himself to raise his head and stop hiding. "Undermining-the-entire-negotiation stupid. I just... got angry and I didn't *think*."

Gamina and Laia exchanged a look—one Addison easily recognized—a wordless agreement that this was certainly not the first time a headstrong decision had gotten him in trouble. It was a wry look, knowing and shadowed with disapproval. But neither woman called him out as their eyes found him once more.

"You'd better tell us what happened," Laia prompted firmly. "There's no point being cryptic. Catastrophizing without details doesn't give us much to work with."

Addison resisted the urge to argue there was no point. That they couldn't help anyway. Instead he squared his shoulders and told them exactly how he had derailed last night's introductions. He spared nothing for the sake of his pride, even as their expressions grew increasingly perplexed.

There may have been amusement hiding beneath the dubious stares, but if so it was artfully concealed.

"You're right," Gamina said when Addison finally tapered off. "That was remarkably stupid." Despite the bluntness of the words, she spoke with a sympathetic tone.

Addison bristled anyway. "Fine. Yes. I made a bad call. Can one of you please explain to me why it's such a huge goddamn deal?"

Both women blinked at him, then exchanged another brief pair of matching looks.

"Which part?" Laia asked.

Addison shook his head, searching for clarity in the frustrated mire of his thoughts. He knew why his misstep was a problem: lying to a potential employer was a disastrous tactic no matter how he came at it. The consequences were direct and obvious, looming immediately over his head. That wasn't where his confusion arose.

"The part where some judgmental old woman gets to talk shit about our captain just because he's a bachelor," he answered at last. "I don't care how much money she's got. Why should she give a damn one way or the other? How is it her business? What's it got to do with whether we can make good on her contract?"

"Oh. Well." Laia set her drink on the table with a soft click. "First, it's *not* her business. And obviously it's ridiculous of her to make it a factor in a contract negotiation, whether it's express or implicit."

Not illegal, though. At least, not any more so than the rest of this ridiculous arrangement. Addison still itched to march back onto the estate and tell Anatoria Baell where she could shove her assumptions.

"She wasn't the only one behaving like it was inconceivable, though," he said. "I mean… Yeah, everyone at that reunion's got plenty of reasons to stay on her good side and say what she wants to hear. But they seemed genuinely surprised. Like they couldn't believe a man Odona's age *wouldn't* have a mate."

"It is… uncommon," Gamina allowed. "Remians generally mate young and mate for life. There are some who think that's how it *should* be. Especially when remaining unattached requires significant effort."

Addison blinked. "What the hell does *that* mean?"

Gamina's mouth twitched at one corner, and Addison tried not to rankle at the fact that he was once again a source of amusement. His question was valid. Plenty of people, especially people who spent their lives constantly on the move, didn't pursue romance. Mating or marriage didn't always fit into a life like theirs. Why should it be so strange for Odona—a captain of his own ship and a man who clearly had other priorities—to postpone or avoid taking a mate?

"You're thinking like a Human," Gamina said as though tracking his exact thoughts. "It's easier for you to set these things aside. Remians contend with... other challenges."

The scowl that had bloomed on Addison's face deepened. "Now who's being cryptic?"

Laia offered a placating smile. "It's a question of biology. Remian adults experience a mating drive once they reach adulthood. Every few years, whether they have a mate or not. It's not dangerous, but it is... uncomfortable. Resisting the imperative is not especially pleasant."

Addison gawped, scowl evaporating from his face as he processed this new information. Coming from anyone but Laia and Gamina, he might suspect he was the butt of a prank.

"It's worse if there's a viable and appealing potential mate close at hand," Laia said. "The situation can exacerbate things. Trigger the mating drive more often. There are plenty of reasons to live isolated on a space ship, but it probably helps in this arena especially."

"Odona is one hundred and seven years old," Gamina added. "The fact that he's never taken a mate is... statistically unlikely. He's an outlier. That doesn't make him wrong. But it does mean he's spent most of his life *consciously choosing* to remain unattached."

"No way," Addison protested, not disbelieving so much as doubting his own perceptions. The only Human among a ship of Remian crew members—how could he miss something so fundamental? "I've lived aboard the *Korria* for seven years. How did I not know this?"

Another look passed between the women, but this one wasn't cryptic at all. Addison could read clearly the arch of Gamina's eyebrow, the barely visible raising of Laia's shoulder, the slow blink of all-black eyes. It was an exchange that said, *Is this too much? Are we meddling? Should we back off?*

Then they looked at him in unison, movements so perfectly matched it seemed practiced.

It was Laia who said, "It makes sense he wouldn't say anything to us. We're his subordinates. And all this... It's private. Not really the kind of thing we speak of openly."

Addison bit his tongue. There was no point arguing that they weren't just Odona's crew; they were his *friends.* The argument wasn't so simple. Odona kept himself deliberately apart in so many ways. As captain, he maintained a careful balance between the personal and the professional. He never shied from expressing affection, but there was a distance too. He'd never asked about Addison's love life; of course Odona had never volunteered information about his own circumstances.

"You don't go around advertising the intricacies of Human biology," Gamina pointed out, light and reasonable.

"No," Addison conceded. Not unless he was actively trying to get laid, which was never a pursuit he shared with his crew mates. He couldn't even picture confiding such things around his captain, couldn't imagine Odona setting foot in one of the noisy dockside dives Addison preferred for his casual connections.

He sat straighter as a different curiosity occurred to him, even though he knew damn well he had no place asking.

"What about Edda? He clearly doesn't have a mate."

"He's young," Gamina said. "It's possible he hasn't been through his first mating drive yet. It's just as possible he hasn't found someone he wants to spend the rest of his life with. His reasons aren't really our business." This time the answer came with a hint of rebuke. A deliberate shutdown, cutting off the torrent of questions Addison still wanted to ask. Gamina's tone made it clear that, no matter how candid the relationship Addison enjoyed with them, they would draw the line at hypothesizing about other people's personal affairs.

Addison subsided, reluctant and a little bit guilty. He'd been invasive enough already. Hell, he'd put Gamina and Laia in an awkward position, asking personal questions. Things Odona especially might not want him to know.

He still could not entirely wrap his head around the fact that he had served for seven years alongside the *Korria's* crew—all Remian—and never known any of this. Yes it was private, but *seven years.* Addison had always prided himself on his observational skills, but maybe his pride had been misplaced.

"Thank you," he said finally, slouching once more into the corner of the couch. "For telling me. I think I understand better now."

"Of course." Gamina smiled at him, a sincere quirk of wide lips. "But if anyone asks? You didn't hear any of this from us."

# Chapter Six

Galin spent the uneventful morning swinging drastically between restless apathy and near panic. He was not a sociable man at the best of times. Stranded on an unfamiliar moon—out of his familiar habitat and surrounded by strangers operating under faulty information—he was nowhere near any sort of best.

His efforts were not helped by the stress of repeatedly fibbing about why his supposed mate was absent. As simple and repetitious as he kept his excuses—his mate didn't travel well, hadn't slept enough last night, needed some extra rest—the need for perfect consistency was a constant drain.

The tour of the city was, he grudgingly admitted, truly impressive. The surface of the moon found unlikely beauty in its patchwork of form and function. Greenery had been grafted onto every available surface, regardless of the angle at which it stood, creating a strange amalgam of architecture and life. Even the industrial buildings—and there were many—stood canvassed by swathes of vining plant life.

This was all just as practical as it was aesthetic, of course. Every square foot of flora helped ease the demands on the oxygen conversion facilities located in every atmospheric dome.

Casting aside pragmatism, the effect was striking. Even better, by pretending to be enthralled by the scope and spectacle of it all, Galin avoided speaking to his fellow guests for a solid hour of Valdez's absence.

He could not avoid interaction completely. Not if he wanted to maintain the illusion of belonging here. There was no dodging every exchange, every friendly curiosity, every idle discussion of local commerce and politics. Galin remembered few names to go with the ever-changing array of faces—Valdez would have done better—but at least he managed not to embarrass himself. He even spotted Karnis Lor across one of the central courtyards when the party returned to the compound. She was too far away for more than a passing wave, and in too much of a hurry to greet properly regardless.

"Karnis hasn't been able to enjoy herself much since arriving." Baell's voice startled him, making his neck twinge from turning his head too fast. He found his host standing to his left, apparently unconcerned with the shock she had just bestowed. She didn't even look at him—too busy peering across the grounds—as she continued. "I'm afraid I don't allow myself to rely on many people. Which means those I *do* trust have to carry more than their share when I delegate."

"I used to find it difficult to delegate at all," Galin admitted, cautious but honest. "It's easier, now that I've found the right crew. I wouldn't remember how to function without them."

"And your mate," Baell said with an air of idle curiosity. "Is he a member of your crew?"

"Of course." No point pretending Valdez didn't work for him. Such a deflection would only render the fiction more difficult to maintain.

If anyone cornered Valdez alone with prying questions, hopefully he would think to remain somewhere near the truth.

"That must be difficult," Baell observed.

They were walking now—Baell setting the pace and Galin remaining in step at her side—following the throng of guests indoors. They kept back just far enough to speak privately as they navigated elaborate hallways, moving with a current comprised entirely of people. Galin didn't know their destination and had no intention of asking.

"Difficult?" he echoed when several silent footsteps didn't help him decipher his host's meaning.

"Being on such intimate terms, yet working closely together." Baell threw him a surprisingly sympathetic look, fleeting but unmistakable in the glare of sunlight from high windows. "I imagine it's a challenge, setting aside your personal feelings and remaining impartial."

Galin laughed, startled and quiet and quick.

It should not have been funny. It *wasn't* funny. Yet there was humor in the fact that Anatoria Baell—who did not know him and was operating under

Valdez's blatant misinformation—could observe something so painfully true.

His feelings *did* make it difficult to maintain the professional distance his relationship with Valdez required. He could afford to be more careless with the others. Keeth, Rielle, even Dak. He could let them closer without fear of impropriety. He had nothing to hide from them.

He could take no such chances with Valdez.

"Yes," he agreed after a heartbeat too long. The truth roughened his voice, pitched it lower than usual. "Very much a challenge. But he is worth it."

No matter how troublesome his own feelings became, he could no longer imagine the *Korria* without Addison Valdez.

Galin blinked as they stepped through an archway and he realized he recognized their destination. It was one of last night's grand halls, a truly massive space with high ceilings and sweeping arches. It was an interior room, no windows whatsoever, but the space still glowed with a pleasant illusion of daylight.

Dozens upon dozens of tables stood in perfect formation across the floor. The tables were circular and low to the ground, with expensive cushions for guests to sit at their designated spaces. No surprise that seating arrangements had not been left to chance. A waitstaff fifty strong subtly assisted guests in finding their places.

When Galin glanced to his side, he discovered Baell had vanished into the crowd. Her absence was a palpable relief.

He considered the small comm unit tucked in a discreet inner pocket of his attire. Valdez had been gone for over four hours, and while Galin wasn't yet worried—Valdez was just as talented in extricating himself from trouble as finding it in the first place— he *was* growing increasingly impatient. Guilty as he felt for exiling Valdez with no explanation last night, he couldn't deny the twist of irritation alongside belated certainty that he should have let Valdez take the damn bed.

Irritation had its place. He resented fending for himself in this ridiculous environment. Valdez had all but invited himself along in the first place; he'd been adamant that Galin needed to bring him, that no one else could do the job half as well. A valid argument, ostensibly. But Valdez couldn't do the job if he *was not here*.

Galin forced his frustration aside as he found and sat in his designated place. An extremely round woman was already sitting on the cushion to his left, her long hair swept back over wide shoulders, a pleasant smile on her soft and pretty face. She was speaking animatedly on something that might have to do with experimental singularity drives, and it was clear she held the entire table in thrall.

The only empty cushion was immediately to Galin's right. And even with the woman on his other side commanding the attention of the table, it was clear Addison's absence had been noticed.

"You must be Galin," the woman said, on reaching what must have been a natural break in her train of thought. "I'm Mallita Denek."

"Delighted," Galin returned with a nod.

"I hope your charming Addison will be joining us," Mallita said. "I've yet to meet him myself, but Nira tells me he entertains some fascinating opinions on cross-sector economic treaties."

He vaguely recalled Valdez taking such a tangent last night, growing heated until Galin set a hand to the nape of his neck and gave a soft squeeze. The gesture had been intended as an admonishment, disguised as a more intimate touch. He didn't remember the name of the person they'd been speaking to at the time, but it could have been Nira.

He offered an apologetic smile and let his gaze drift to acknowledge the entire table. "I hope so. He never sleeps well the first night off-ship, no matter how perfect the accommodations. Believe me, when he woke this morning he wasn't fit for company. But he promised to join us when he feels better."

Drinks appeared at the table by the magic of well-trained waitstaff, most of the glasses filled with a sparkling ale that Galin now knew—from the detailed tour of the city—was produced locally on Falaris. He took a polite sip before setting the glass aside. A matching beverage stood in front of the empty space Valdez should have occupied; Galin had requested a drink for him in a burst of optimism.

He hoped, selfishly and fervently, that his optimism would prove out.

At least Mallita offered boisterous company as the luncheon progressed. She seemed happy to hold court and demanded very little by way of response. The rest of the table watched her with nearly identical expressions of devotion and admiration. Every one of them—men, women, and other—gave the unmistakable impression of being completely smitten, and Mallita clearly enjoyed the reverence. Here was a woman accustomed to being the center of attention and more than capable of holding her ground.

"Now then." Mallita turned to look directly at Galin as soup bowls were cleared away to make room for the next course. Unexpected purpose flashed in her eyes. "I dearly hope you won't think I'm too forward, but I sense *such* a connection between us. I feel like I can ask you anything."

Galin's skin prickled with apprehension, and with the abrupt certainty that he had not been assigned this seat by chance.

"Tell me about your— What was his name? Addison?" A canny spark glinted in her eyes, and Galin sincerely doubted she'd managed to forget Valdez's name in such a short span. "How, in all our strange universe, did you come to take a Human for a mate? And one so *young*! Why, he can't even be fifty years old!"

Galin did not bother to confirm Valdez's age, nor did he point out that the Human lifespan ran far shorter than a Remian's average years.

He couldn't dodge the interrogation entirely. He didn't need Valdez's quick wit to recognize just how purposeful these questions were. Baell had almost certainly arranged this seating in order to gather information. If not about the veracity of the story— she hadn't seemed suspicious during their short walk together—then at least as to Galin's manner and person. Even here he needed to comport himself well. Mallita would almost certainly report back to Baell on whether he made a favorable impression.

The problem—and it was a damnably large problem—centered on the fact that Galin could not sustain a credible lie.

But perhaps the truth would suffice if he told it very, very carefully. He could embellish. He had already imbued some honesty to their story in his conversation with Baell. He would simply have to warn Valdez to do the same, and pray he didn't have an opportunity to cook up more fanciful fictions before they reunited.

"Addison is... complicated," he said after what he hoped was a reasonable pause to gather his thoughts.

"He's been a member of my crew for almost seven years, and I'm sure you can imagine the unique trials *that* has presented."

Mallita made a sound of agreement and took a sip of her drink, freshly topped off by a passing server. Her expression, eyes wide and piercing, called for him to continue.

Galin downed a generous swallow of his own drink to stall for time. His mind spun in an effort to find something to say that he could bear putting into words for a table of complete strangers.

There was no point explaining the position Valdez occupied among the *Korria's* crew. For one thing, with the possible exception of Mallita, no one at this table cared about the intricacies of Galin's business methods. For another, it wasn't as though he had any concise way to describe the myriad roles fulfilled by one improbable Human. Communications expert, financial strategist, legal consultant, bookkeeper. All things Galin had managed just fine on his own before Addison Valdez came along.

They were all things he managed far better, and far faster, with Valdez at his side. Barely two years had passed aboard the *Korria* before Valdez graduated— mostly by force of stubbornness—from glorified assistant to indispensable component of Galin's business process, and no one else on the crew had breathed a single word of complaint.

"I knew the moment he came aboard that he was special," Galin admitted at last, self-conscious in his honesty. "It took me a few years to recognize just *how* special. By the time I realized I had a problem, I could no longer imagine my life without him."

Valdez had been uncomfortably young when he first joined Galin's crew. He'd been a rescue. A passenger they intended to leave behind at the first safe port of call. An adult by the measurement of most governments, but still young enough to inspire only a faint and affectionate protectiveness in the *Korria's* crew and captain. A stranger. An outsider. Temporary.

That hadn't lasted. Valdez had, against all odds, *stayed*. Worse, he'd grown up. More steady, more comfortable in his own skin, more sure of himself aboard Galin's small ship. And one day Galin had looked at him—looked at the Human he'd never intended to hire in the first place—and understood he wanted things he could never admit to.

The problem did not lie in Valdez's youth. He was a grown man, for all that he was a quarter Galin's age. But Galin was the *Korria's* captain. The topmost authority among a small band of loyal employees. He took care of his crew.

He did not dare express feelings that might be unwelcome. He would never forgive himself for putting any of them in an untenable position, and admitting such an interest in Valdez would be untenable indeed.

"Not such a problem after all," Mallita observed with a broad smile. "It's clear he adores you, and that you feel the same."

Galin forced a smile of his own past the wistful ache her words raised in his chest.

Again he forced himself to speak an uncomfortable truth, painful, but better than a lie he couldn't sell. "He means everything to me."

Mallita's gaze cut upward an instant before a hand closed on Galin's shoulder. Galin startled even as his senses registered the familiar weight. He turned his head, tilted up to see exactly what he should have expected: Valdez standing behind him. Watchful and attentive.

"Did I miss anything important?" A soft, strange smile touched Valdez's expressive face.

The hand fell from Galin's shoulder as Valdez lowered himself gracefully to the floor, settling onto the empty pillow and folding his legs in front of him. A moment later and Valdez's hand reached atop the table, fingers sliding almost delicately over Galin's hand and wrist.

"Just the first three courses," Galin managed to answer. He sounded only a little choked, startlement tucked away as he forced himself to meet Valdez's eyes. He felt uncomfortably exposed, and even though he wasn't sure he wanted to know, he heard himself ask, "How long were you standing there?"

"Long enough." The soft smile took on a sheepish edge. "*Complicated*, huh?"

Galin closed his eyes for only a second, and when he opened them he scrounged a smile from some desperate recess. "You know as well as I do that *complicated* is an understatement where you are concerned."

Valdez smiled wider and took his hand back, claiming Galin's drink on the way—Valdez's glass had been cleared away by staff when he failed to appear—and downing a generous swallow. Genuine amusement lit his face as he lowered the glass, and the expression set off wild relief in Galin's chest. Valdez would not be nearly so entertained if he recognized the earnest feeling in Galin's confessions.

Galin pretended not to bristle beneath the attention of the entire table. Too many eyes, black and glinting and curious, were watching their exchange. He plucked his drink out of Valdez's hand, brushing their fingers together in the process. It was the closest he could bring himself to the sort of territorial gesture that would declare Valdez his mate in front of their audience. Something more blatant would have been better, certainly. But Galin felt too much on display already.

"Did you save me any dessert?" Valdez asked.

"We haven't even reached dessert."

"Perfect." Valdez beamed, flashing that brilliant smile for the entire table to see.

Galin's chest warmed at the sight, as it always did, and for once he made no attempt to keep the rush of affection from his face. Thorny as this farce was, surely he could show this one sliver of weakness without giving himself away.

\*

The rest of the meal remained uneventful, with Valdez alternately charming Mallita and fading into the background of other people's conversations. More than once he stole food from Galin's plate, even though the dishes served were identical in every observable way. A habit that seemed, improbably, intended to broadcast their connection. A Human quirk, perhaps. Galin couldn't ask in front of so many meddlesome witnesses.

There were even more activities to attend after lunch. Dull but well planned out, games and socializing and even a professional dance troupe. At least more of the faces surrounding them were familiar now. Galin still couldn't tell if he was making a positive impression on anyone, least of all Anatoria Baell.

At every turn he felt out of his element, stiff and uncomfortable. Certain he was about to say something wrong and give away the truth.

At least Valdez remained at his side through the rest of the day. For all that he didn't apologize for disappearing, his attitude since returning seemed contrite. He never wandered away for more than a few minutes at a time. There was something almost solicitous in the way he stood pressed along Galin's side, arm around his waist, carrying the conversation whenever discussions encircled them too directly to deflect.

Valdez seemed so at ease that Galin began to forget how strange it was to be sharing this space. He grew accustomed to the sturdy presence of narrow shoulders beneath his arm. When tentative fingers touched his hand, he no longer had to suppress his surprise, despite the intimacy of the gesture. It felt unexpectedly natural. Normal. *Right*, in a way he did not dare dwell on.

By the time night fell and the guests began to disperse, Galin felt... Not comfortable exactly. He couldn't risk enjoying Valdez's proximity. It would be far too easy to take advantage of their shared pretense, which meant comfort was not a milestone he had any hope of achieving. But there was *something* there. An unexpected familiarity. Unasked for, but present just the same.

He banished such thoughts to the back of his mind as he and Valdez bid the other guests goodnight.

Their assigned rooms had been cleaned in their absence, every piece of fabric folded and surfaces polished to an unnecessary shine.

Galin glanced around as the door sealed shut behind them. "I hope you put the extra blankets on the bed before you left this morning." He hadn't considered the appearance of things at the time. He'd been far too distracted by the acidic way Valdez glared through him, at the biting refusal to attend the morning's itinerary.

"I did." Valdez crossed the room and pressed a panel to darken the window, blocking out the night-covered skyline and making the room feel cozy, if a little claustrophobic. "I figured we wouldn't want to manufacture an argument bad enough for you to kick me out of bed, and Baell's staff would *definitely* have ratted us out if they found anything amiss in our rooms."

"Agreed," Galin murmured. He slid open the bedroom door, undoing the top fastenings of his shirt collar as he stepped over the threshold. The light level in the room rose automatically with his entrance.

Valdez followed a step behind him, hovering in the doorframe and peering at him with watchful eyes.

"That was some impressive storytelling, sir."

Galin turned, curious and confused. "What storytelling?"

Valdez gave a wry snort and crossed his arms, leaning one shoulder against the edge of the open door. "Right. Sorry. Too many hours ago. I meant at lunch. All that stuff you said about how we met. How you knew. That was damn good. I've never seen you lie so smoothly before."

Ice chilled the length of Galin's spine, but he did his best to keep his posture loose, his expression bland. Valdez wasn't calling him out. He wore no air of skepticism. He seemed genuinely impressed with Galin's performance in the dining hall—clearly certain it *had been* a performance—and as long as Galin played along they would be fine.

"I don't plan on making a habit of it," he said before the quiet could stretch too long. Then, glancing across the tiny bedroom, "You should take the bed tonight. I'll manage with a couple blankets and the floor."

Valdez gawped at him from the open doorframe. His eyes, always full of enough white to be startling, were wider than ever as he stared at Galin in disbelief.

"You can't be serious," Valdez said at last.

"Why not?"

"It's just... not fair, that's why. This situation isn't any *less* my fault today than it was last night." Valdez straightened from his slouch but kept his arms crossed tightly over his chest. "I told you the settee was fine."

Galin scoffed, amusement kindling in his chest despite the ludicrous disagreement. "You looked like you were trying to set me on fire with your mind while you said it."

In their years working closely together, he'd observed Valdez deprived of sleep plenty of times. Even so, this morning had been a sight to behold. Considering it had been Galin's fault he'd slept so terribly—the piece of furniture certainly did not look inviting—the reaction seemed reasonable enough.

They couldn't repeat the same sleeping arrangements. Galin would feel far too guilty come morning, even if Valdez did a better job masking his sleepless ire. The bed *should* have accommodated both of them—it was more than large enough—and it wasn't fair for Galin to make his companion suffer simply because he didn't trust his own heart to behave.

"Sir," Valdez began to protest.

"The settee is clearly *not* fine," Galin cut him decisively off. He injected firm command into his voice, making it clear the subject was not up for negotiation.

"This is stupid. We should just share."

"Take the bed," Galin ordered. Valdez could wonder at his obstinacy, but so long as he didn't reach the correct conclusions everything would be fine.

Galin had no intention of explaining why they could not share. It may have been a ridiculous line of demarcation, but he needed to maintain it just the same. Never mind that the bed was easily wide enough for them to take separate sides and be nowhere near touching. He still could not cross this line.

Not when his own feelings were so distractingly inappropriate; and not when Valdez had no idea.

"*Take the bed*," Galin repeated with unyielding finality. "I'll be all right on the floor."

He made for the washroom a moment later, the line of his back and the closing door effectively ending the discussion.

*Chapter Seven*

Addison woke to daylight—open blinds—and a fuzzy sense that he'd had pleasant dreams.

There was something inexpressibly luxurious about waking up this way. Sprawled beneath thin blankets, groggy and lazy and comfortable. No chilly spaceship air, no perpetual darkness, no bunk so narrow only the raised railing along the edge prevented him from rolling to the floor from turbulence or a restless night.

It took him a moment to realize the glimpse of sky through the window meant Odona must already be up. Probably waiting for him—Addison needed to get moving—to find his captain and set a better precedent than the day before.

Addison eased sluggishly upright, bracing his palms against the mattress and tilting his head in a lazy stretch. A glance confirmed: the door between bedroom and sitting room was open and the floor beyond was empty. Odona had folded his blankets and placed them on the foot of the bed, had replaced the pillow too.

Belatedly Addison noticed the rhythm of water through the washroom wall, which answered the question of where Odona had gone. Here too was an unaccustomed luxury: a shower with *actual water.*

Tame next to the opulence he'd already witnessed, but it still felt extravagant. The sonic showers aboard the *Korria* got the job done, but they didn't feel nearly as good as a proper sluice of hot water along bare skin.

If Odona was still in the shower, Addison saw no rush to get his own ass out of this gloriously comfortable bed. Despite the stream of light through the window, the chronometer beside the door proclaimed the hour so early it barely constituted 'morning.'

He flopped back down again, pillow squashing beneath his head as he settled with a sigh.

By the time the water cut off and the washroom door slid open, Addison had nearly dozed off again. He blinked idly at the sound of the wardrobe opening, the faint rustle of luggage and fabric.

The vestiges of sleep vanished in a flash of attentiveness as Addison's gaze landed on his captain. Odona wore an enormous towel wrapped at his waist, but the rest of him was bare, dark skin striking alongside pale fabric. The broad line of his back and shoulders moved smoothly as he gathered his clothes, the muscles of his arms working as he hefted and put away his suitcase. When he turned enough for Addison to see him in profile, the view was even more distracting. Softness and strength in perfect proportion.

Perhaps Addison could blame dazed sleepiness for the fact that it took him so long to realize he was staring. Fuck, this was invasive as hell. In all his years aboard the *Korria*, he'd never seen Odona so very close to naked. He had no right whatsoever to this unexpectedly intimate view.

Even after seven years aboard the *Korria*, Addison was barely familiar with Remian physiology. He'd seen plenty of other species undressed, but his knowledge of the Remian body was almost entirely abstract. Here, now, this fleeting glimpse seared itself into his brain in an instant. Odona's stocky torso was comprised of powerful muscles and softer edges—not so different from a Human of similar stature—but the muscles themselves aligned differently, creating unfamiliar shapes and shadows beneath bare skin. Sturdy thickness balanced perfectly with distractingly long limbs.

Odona's back was turned to him again, and Addison used the opportunity to shift his weight silently on the mattress. Facing the opposite direction and closing his eyes. He did his damnedest not to let his mind linger anywhere inappropriate.

His eyes were still closed when a firm hand shook his shoulder.

Odona stood directly in front of him now, between the bed and window. Addison blinked up into his face, though it was difficult to read his expression. Odona's silhouette blocked out most of the sun from the window, but Addison could still tell he'd chosen a lighter suit today. It was the same stiff fabric—same high collar, same crisp lines and long sleeves and perfectly shaped contours—but this time in a paler gray, almost blue in direct light.

It looked damn good.

"Good morning." Odona withdrew his hand and stepped back, regarding Addison with patient humor. "Did you sleep any better last night?"

"Yes." Addison had slept beautifully last night. Better than he usually did in his own bed aboard the *Korria. Exponentially better* than he'd managed on that damn settee. He felt rested and ready. Eager, even, to spend another day spinning plausible fictions. It was a task rendered easier than expected thanks to Odona's tendency to simply tell the truth whenever possible.

Odona had proven capable of more elaborate lies. Addison still couldn't believe the cryptic yet convincingly heartfelt story he'd overheard the day before. But given the chance, Odona clearly preferred blunt and simple truth. Amazing how many details of their normal life fit effortlessly into the scenario Addison had constructed around them.

"Did you sleep okay?" Addison kicked the blankets aside as he sat up.

"Well enough."

Looking more closely now, Addison took in the lines of Odona's face. He looked tired. Not set-the-city-on-fire-and-burn-it-down tired, like Addison had felt the morning before, but still rough around the edges. There were shadows smudging his expression, making those all-black eyes look darker than ever.

Addison bit his tongue and didn't comment on the obvious signs of fatigue. He would need to come up with some new argument this evening. They had two more nights to survive on this estate. Addison sure as hell wasn't volunteering to sleep on the floor—though it must be better than any of the furniture in the other room—but it didn't seem fair for Odona to remain in exile either. Whatever Odona's hang-up, surely Addison could convince him this standoff was ridiculous.

He wouldn't win the battle now, though. He had no fresh ammunition, and he wasn't awake enough to present his case convincingly.

"What's today's itinerary?" he asked as he rose from the bed and made his own way to the washroom door. Despite the plethora of information he'd studied before they reached Falaris, he had little idea what to expect day-to-day. Baell seemed to enjoy keeping her guests on their toes, announcing activities on a pronounced delay. Or perhaps she only kept the information from Addison and Odona. A deliberate challenge as part of their unorthodox audition.

It was a remarkably plausible theory.

This was, without contest, the strangest contract negotiation Addison had ever experienced.

Odona perched on the un-mussed side of the bed as Addison ducked through the washroom door without bothering to close it behind him. Around the corner, he could undress and step into the shower without being seen, but still hear what Odona might say.

"A lengthy cruise on Lake Laris," Odona answered, sounding confounded by the entire prospect. "Food and drink served aboard the vessel, of course. Anatoria Baell wouldn't want her guests to go hungry while admiring the largest artificial lake in the solar system."

Addison snorted as he tossed his loose sleep clothes to the floor. "Heaven forfend. She won't expect us to swim, will she?"

"Can you imagine this crowd submerging themselves in a lake, artificial or not?" Odona retorted. "Besides which, there's apparently quite a bit of aquatic life, much of it dangerous. Swimming is not encouraged."

Addison touched the panel beside the shower partition to activate a steady flow of water from the ceiling, pitching his voice louder to be heard over the steady patter. "Is this an all-day affair?"

"No." Odona's voice also rose to be heard over the water. "There's something else planned for the evening, immediately after the cruise. I've no idea what it is. When I tried to ask a member of Baell's staff, they refused to give me a straight answer."

"What, not even a hint?" Addison was only half listening, half savoring the water warming his skin. There were small bottles arrayed along a narrow ledge near shoulder level, identical in shape but with contents a variety of colors. No labels. He picked one up and opened it. The contents looked and smelled about right for shampoo, so he poured some into his palm.

It *felt* like shampoo too, lathering into his hair easily. Even this seemed luxurious and unnecessary. He couldn't remember the last time he'd used *wet shampoo* on his hair, not to mention anything that smelled this good. His usual products were practical, nondescript, and virtually scentless. This was better.

Odona's voice still carried to him, but standing directly beneath the cascade of water made it more challenging to follow as his captain continued.

"They did suggest wearing comfortable footwear and clothing we don't mind sweating in."

Addison began rinsing his hair and didn't answer until his head was no longer submerged. "I'm guessing this event's just as optional as the rest?"

"If by 'optional' you mean that we will both be there smiling the entire time," Odona retorted without rancor, "then yes. Tonight's mysterious exertion is entirely optional."

The washroom was warm enough that Addison felt perfectly comfortable as he stepped from the shower and deactivated the spray; but he still regretted removing himself from the absolute heaven of steaming hot water.

"We'll have a chance to change between the cruise and the exertion, right? Fuck, did we even *bring* comfortable footwear?" He grabbed a towel—hanging conveniently beside the shower—and began to squeeze the excess water from his hair. He let the rest of his body air dry, dripping all over the smooth tile floor without concern.

"I'm sure we've got something. Dak managed all the supply acquisitions. He's not one to leave contingencies unconsidered."

"No," Addison agreed. "He really isn't." Edda Dak was the most meticulous member of a detail-oriented crew. He'd have left nothing to chance. If there was a need he couldn't foresee, Anatoria Baell would almost certainly have some sort of contingency plan ready.

Addison left off drying his still-damp hair and draped the towel about his waist. He grabbed his now slightly dampened sleepwear from the floor. He should follow the more finicky beauty routine that would allow him to wear his hair down—Edda had assured him it was a more striking and appropriate look for the company they were dealing with—but surely allowing it to air dry without styling this once wouldn't be the failure that cost them the contract. Besides, if the day ahead involved a lake cruise and physically taxing activities, he wanted his hair *up*. Tugged into the tight queue he preferred regardless. He hoped like hell Edda had packed at least a few of the thin leather cords Addison needed to tie his hair back.

Of course he had. Contingencies.

Odona was no longer sitting on the edge of the bed when Addison emerged from the washroom. He'd relocated instead to stand near the window, hands clasped at his back and gaze turned outward across the grounds.

"Don't just stand there," Addison teased as he tossed his sleep clothes onto the rumpled bed and began to dig for whatever outfit he was supposed to wear today. "See if Ruke Hall's got a kitchen that will send up *actual coffee*."

"Already done," Odona answered without turning from the window. When Addison threw a quick glance over his bare shoulder, he saw Odona's posture was drawn inexplicably tense. "No coffee, I'm afraid. But I requested two mugs of ruhn with breakfast."

Ruhn must have been what they drank the morning before. An acceptable substitute, much as Addison would've preferred his usual vice. He paused as the rest of the statement registered.

"Breakfast?" he asked.

"Breakfast," Odona repeated deliberately. "I thought we might skip the crowd and eat in peace for once, hopefully without displeasing our host. We'll be trapped on a boat with most of these people for a significant portion of the day. Surely even Anatoria Baell can't begrudge us a brief interlude of privacy."

Addison breathed a noncommittal sound—a quiet interval did sound appealing—and finally settled on an outfit and began to dress.

\*

The lake, it turned out, was truly enormous. Baell had commissioned a spectacle, and the result was impressive. The glassy surface stretched to such distances that it was difficult to see the shore from the massive, multi-tiered vessel gliding across the water.

The vastness stretched even farther straight ahead—a waterway so long Addison could clearly discern where the dome structure high above swept low and met with another quadrant—a second dome.

The vessel itself was like nothing Addison had ever seen. Tall and bulky, but also tapering to a narrow shape at the front. Its prow stretched long and thin as it cut a path through the water. Alongside the hull, the vessel's wake shone with shivering jewel tones. Blue and green and purple.

It was a beautiful spectacle. Addison couldn't complain about the view.

The company seemed more relaxed as well, thanks in no small part to the open bar on the central deck. Addison hadn't partaken—and he knew Odona was abstaining too—but the generous quantity of alcohol turned the stiff-backed, prying, affluent dupes on this boat into... not *better* conversationalists, exactly. But somehow more pleasant. Less likely to catch on if Addison or Odona slipped up in their narrative.

The alcohol also meant Baell's guests were, on the whole, less circumspect. With the rigid edges of decorum softened, different attitudes emerged. Flirtations became more blatant, and eyes roved far less subtly than they'd done even during the opening festivities. Not just over him, Addison realized, but occasionally over Odona. Mates and spouses of guests—at least Addison hoped no one directly related to Anatoria Baell would look at Odona that way under the circumstances—hanging primly on their companions' arms while ogling without shame.

Hell, maybe it wasn't just the alcohol. Maybe here, now, a couple days into the reunion, people were more comfortable loosening up. Addison couldn't be sure, and he didn't particularly care.

It didn't really matter why their fellow guests were more at ease, or why they felt at liberty to drink more heavily. What mattered was the practical effect. Admiring stares didn't bother Addison where he himself was concerned. He knew he was a novelty, one of very few Humans amid the crowd; and for all his complaining about the clothing Edda had acquired, he *knew* he looked good.

No, what bothered him was the way lingering eyes followed his captain.

Odona took no apparent notice, but Addison knew him too well to be fooled. Odona did not like being the center of attention. He would certainly not appreciate the way the other guests watched him. Idle observation in most cases, but still rude considering the lack of shame or pretense.

It was all the worse for the fact that, so far as everyone on this boat knew, the two of them were together. Both of them spoken for. Unavailable. Gamina had said Remians tended to mate for life, which meant these near-strangers had no business eyeing Odona up like this. Holding eye contact too long, smiling a little too intimately, twining suggestiveness into every wordless signal.

Addison was not prepared for the fact that all this made him *angry*. But then, why shouldn't he be angry? As far as any of these people knew, Odona was his, and they could stay the hell away from Addison's mate unless they wanted a confrontation on their hands. Surely he was justified in taking offense.

Baell probably wouldn't appreciate a standoff. Despite the fact that he'd only seen her fleetingly so far today, Addison had no doubts the staff would alert her if there were an incident

So Addison did the next best thing. Short of throwing diplomacy to the wind, he remained stubbornly in Odona's orbit. Even when his more restless instincts urged him to wander, he stayed put. Directly at Odona's side where he belonged. He remained close enough to touch—and to be touched—to accept and reciprocate the soft but calculated slide of fingers against his own.

In return, Odona made a point of touching him when anyone looked too greedily at Addison, a charming and almost convincing show of possessiveness.

Addison had no explanation for the thrill that ran along his spine every time this happened. He sure as hell wasn't entitled to enjoy the warmth in Odona's hands—just like he had no business acknowledging what a distracting figure his captain cut in that damn outfit—but he couldn't shake the reaction. It was... nice. Pleasant. Odona touched him so rarely on the ship, a fact Addison had noticed but never spent much effort considering. There was something unexpectedly satisfying in being held so close, even if it was only a complicated pretext.

It was probably inevitable when, following the departure of an especially friendly young couple, Addison's irrational jealousy surged too sharply to be ignored.

"I wish they'd all stop looking at you like that," he muttered, arm tightening where it rested around Odona's waist. "Those two looked like they wanted to invite you back to their rooms tonight."

Odona laughed, a quiet but startled burst. "They did give that impression."

"Who the fuck do they think they are?" Addison hissed, his temper not at all calmed by the obvious show of amusement. "You're *my* mate. I'm standing *right here*."

When he tilted his head back, he found Odona's expression had fallen serious. Narrowed black eyes glinted with curiosity, and there was confusion in the deep furrow at the very center of Odona's brow.

"Sorry." Addison's face flushed, embarrassment over his outburst heating his skin. "I'm being ridiculous."

He was *not* Odona's mate, and it was absurd to take offense. He didn't need to know these people. He didn't need their respect—only Anatoria Baell's—and none of this should matter. Whatever slight he might feel at being disregarded at Odona's side, it wasn't as though he had grounds for jealousy. Hell, Odona clearly had no trouble ignoring the people giving Addison similar attention. Up until now, Odona's bland, blank expression had not faltered once.

It was faltering now, but that probably had more to do with Addison's tantrum than with the other guests.

In a surprisingly smooth maneuver, Odona pulled Addison around a corner and onto a narrow patch of deck that seemed more like an afterthought than a design choice. It placed them effectively out of view from the main deck, and when Odona dropped his arm from around Addison's shoulders, Addison took a grudging step away.

Strange to suddenly have personal space again, after hours at close range. It should have been a relief. Instead it made Addison feel jittery, not to mention uncomfortably aware of the piercing chill of the wind.

Odona watched him with obvious concern, ever the perceptive captain. "Are you all right?"

"Just getting tired of all this bullshit."

The look Odona gave him then was wry and sharp and disbelieving, eyebrows arching impossibly high on his handsome face. The look wasn't accusatory so much as sardonic, pointed in a way that left Addison little doubt as to the source of the vexation.

"I don't mean the part where I'm hanging off your arm pretending you're the love of my life." Addison barely resisted the urge to roll his eyes. "I just mean... *them*. All of them. They're so pushy and entitled. There are at least a dozen I'd shove off this boat if I were sure they wouldn't get eaten by lake monsters." He was reasonably certain they wouldn't be hurt regardless. There were bound to be plenty of redundant safety protocols on a vessel like this. And it would be satisfying as hell to see some of the more infuriating guests gasping and treading water in their finery, furious and soaked to the skin.

Odona sounded only slightly strained when he answered, "We only have to put up with them for another couple days. Or until Baell decides to cut to the chase and make us an offer."

Addison turned toward the high railing that ran along the edge of the deck, folding his arms over the metal bar and sweeping his eyes across the horizon. He could just see a sliver of shore from here. Sunlight glinted on what might have been buildings in the distance.

"Do you think she's warming up to us?" Addison hadn't really spoken to her since that first disastrous opening reception.

"Honestly?" Odona mirrored his pose, leaning on the railing to Addison's left. Not quite close enough for their arms to touch. "I have no idea. She certainly believes this story of yours. I spoke to her yesterday, and I doubt she would've been shy about calling out any lingering suspicions."

"But she didn't say anything about the contract?" Addison's eyes narrowed even though he was still staring across the smooth surface of the lake.

"Not a word. Maybe that's a good thing. If she'd already rejected our proposal, surely she wouldn't string us along. Why keep us here if she's not seriously considering us for the job?"

"I guess." Addison wished like hell he felt more confident in his answer. For now he had to settle for the fact that it was a reasonable conclusion, and that Odona wasn't prone to unfounded optimism.

"You can stay out of sight for a while if you need to," Odona said, in a voice so quiet Addison barely deciphered the words over the whipping wind.

When he turned his head he found Odona peering down into his face with an unexpectedly soft expression. Sympathy—that much was easy to parse—but also something else Addison couldn't quite read.

"I'm fine," he protested, rankling a little at the idea of shirking his responsibilities again.

One corner of Odona's mouth twitched, faint movement drawing Addison's attention away from dark eyes. Amusement seemed an unlikely reaction to their present conversation, but Addison couldn't explain the not-quite-a-smile any other way. He raised his eyes again, glowering now as he met Odona's piercing look.

"Of course you're fine." The agreement should have sounded patronizing, but somehow Odona made it sound completely sincere. His weight shifted, and he braced one elbow on the railing so that he could face Addison directly. "But you've also been taking the brunt of all this for hours. It's draining work. And considering you've gone the entire time without threatening to push anyone overboard, I'd say you deserve a break."

Humor cracked through Addison's defensiveness, and he snorted aloud at the echo of his own previous sentiment. He *hadn't* threatened to push anyone overboard. Not to their faces. But he'd just admitted to considering it.

The look they exchanged then was a complicated thing, pursed lips and narrowed eyes, amusement stifled beneath more immediate pressures. Years of working closely together, of shared challenges, of mutual exasperation and respect, all wrapped into one fleeting moment that passed silent and expressive between them.

"Do you want me to bring you a drink?" Odona asked.

"No. Thanks. But if you really don't mind, I would like to hide out here for a while. Just until I can be really sure I won't put anyone in the lake."

"Of course."

Then Odona was gone, and Addison found himself alone in his obscure corner of the deck. Surrounded by solitude, but not quiet. There was too much wind and too much muffled noise carrying around the corner from the main deck.

He let his eyes unfocus, and the horizon blurred as he allowed his thoughts to wander and evaporate. He did his damnedest not to think as the vessel rode efficiently along the water. It was a beautiful panorama. When he sharpened his gaze and squinted straight up into the sky, he could just make out the gridwork that shaped the dome high overhead.

"Enjoying the view?"

Addison startled. He hadn't noticed Anatoria Baell's approach, too lost in his detached and meandering thoughts. She stepped into the space directly beside him, exactly where Odona had been standing... How long ago? Ten minutes? Twenty? Addison honestly didn't know how long he'd been hiding back here. He was almost certainly overdue to rejoin Odona.

But he could hardly do so now. Baell stood in his way. She curled one hand around the railing, gripped the top of her cane loosely with the other, and regarded him with untempered curiosity. Her dark-through eyes flashed with questions that would probably raise every last one of Addison's hackles, but he forced himself to give her a welcoming smile.

"It's a beautiful landscape," he said. "Hard to believe it was constructed by architects and not nature."

"I had a hand in the design myself," Baell said. The words were matter-of-fact. An assertion that should have sounded boastful, but delivered with such blunt self-assurance it felt anything but. Then, apparently uninterested in waiting for praise, she spoke again, this time with the firm weight of command. "Tell me about Galin Odona."

Addison startled again, blinking up at Baell's sternly lined face.

It didn't feel like a trap, but he couldn't guess what sort of answer she was looking for. Something to do with his business acumen? His reliability as an employer and transporter of challenging merchandise? Or was she after something more personal?

"What do you want to know?"

"Anything you're inclined to share," she answered benignly, though her intent expression said she was after something more specific. When Addison only stared at her—exaggerating his confusion in the hopes of clearer guidance—she tilted her head closer in a conspiratorial gesture. "Please don't take this the wrong way, but you two... You make for an unlikely pair. It's clear he adores you, and your own devotion is unmistakable. But Galin Odona is not the most expressive man. So I come to you instead, because I would like to understand."

Addison bristled.

"What is there to understand?" He couldn't entirely quiet the defensiveness that crept into his tone.

Baell did not look taken aback by the demand. If anything she looked *more* amused than she had a moment before, and Addison bit his tongue to keep from snarling a thoughtless retort. After a moment Baell simply tucked a flyaway strand of hair behind her ear—making no acknowledgment of Addison's ire—and leaned more heavily on her cane.

"Perhaps 'understand' is the wrong word," she said. "I'm just curious. How you met. How you came to realize you were something more than colleagues. Surely you can forgive an old woman her harmless curiosities."

They weren't harmless. They were prying and personal. But then, Addison was the one who had made this personal in the first place.

"I've worked with him for seven years." He let go of his irritation with difficulty, softening his voice by degrees. "It didn't take much of that to figure out I wanted more. It took him a while longer to come around, but we figured it out." He left it at that. Tempting as it was to spin a complicated story, for once he decided to keep his mouth shut. Keep it short. He would follow Odona's example and let Baell fill in her own blanks, make her own assumptions.

"He's vastly older than you."

"I don't care about that." Easy enough to inject fervent conviction into the statement. "Hell, he's also got double my lifespan. Why not level the ground a little? Besides, have you *looked* at him? Who wouldn't want more of that?"

*Honestly*, who wouldn't? He'd never looked at Odona quite so deliberately before, but he *had looked*. He'd been looking even harder since arriving at Baell's estate. Unintended consequences. He set those thoughts aside for the time being. They were none of Baell's concern, and Addison did not need them to sell this story.

"And the fact that he's your captain?"

"Okay. Yeah. The fact he's my captain gets a little complicated." Addison couldn't very well argue otherwise and maintain a convincing lie. He could imagine a romantic relationship with Galin Odona— hell, he could imagine it more easily now than he would have a few days ago—but in no variation was there a simple answer to balancing the personal and professional.

"How do you manage it?" Baell asked. "My own mate... I never let him work for me, for fear of uglying our marriage with business-related disagreements. I can't imagine *beginning* with business and then choosing a different path."

The candor caught Addison off guard. He knew Anatoria Baell was a widow. Logically that meant she'd had a mate once. But to hear her actually talk about it? To hear her admit to the complexities of an actual relationship? That was entirely strange and unexpected.

"We try to keep everything as separate as we can. Work is work. The rest is us." He turned, staring once more across the shimmering lake. "I wouldn't trade it for anything. There is *literally* nowhere in the galaxy I'd rather be." This too he allowed to carry the heavier weight of truth. So he and Odona weren't really a couple—so what? He still meant it. Seven years ago he'd boarded the *Korria*, a stray and a pity case. Some days he still couldn't believe they'd let him stay.

He was a whole lot better off now. Odona paid his employees well, and Addison had been smart with his money. He could leave. Go almost anywhere and get a new start.

But he didn't want to. The thought of leaving his small adoptive family put a quiet ache behind his ribs. The thought of leaving *Odona* made his entire chest hurt. This wasn't new knowledge, but it hit him hard just the same. Left him scrambling to ground himself as he sought the words to answer Baell's curiosity.

"Galin is a good man," he said without looking at her. He saw no point pretending this wasn't about business when they both knew this nudging interrogation—personal as it might seem—came down to a very specific purpose. "He takes good care of his crew, and he takes good care of *me*. Whatever you're looking for in all this, I hope you find it. He'll do right by you as a business partner."

When he glanced to his side, he couldn't read either approval or disapproval on her face. Her considering expression offered only a measured, deliberate blank. Carefully crafted to give nothing away.

When she spoke, her tone was equally measured. "Thank you, young man. I'll consider your advice."

Then she gave a tight nod, an even tighter smile, and disappeared the way she'd come, vanishing around the corner and leaving Addison once more alone.

# Chapter Eight

They spent hours on the lake. Time passed without hurry, guests enjoying food and drink and conversation. As mid-afternoon came on, so did an unexpected dusk.

Galin had been making no effort to track their direction or progress across the water, beyond taking notice whenever they passed from one dome to another. It had happened three times. Anatoria Baell's lake truly was a wonder.

Valdez must have noticed his confusion, because Galin didn't even have to ask his question aloud. Valdez's explanation came earnest and complete: thanks to a quirk of the moon's rotation, a stripe near the equator never received any direct sunlight.

They must be approaching that area now, judging by the way darkness was steadily encroaching, fast and far ahead of schedule. The other guests took notice, commented idly, but moved on to other topics without concern. More gossip, more business, more bragging and back-patting.

By the time the vessel docked alongside the shore, ending the cruise and allowing the passengers to disembark, Galin was thoroughly finished with all things social.

He felt exhausted, not physically but in every other way. Mentally, emotionally, diplomatically. Hell, in that moment he would've given almost anything to excuse himself back to the estate. Maybe take a long run along the more discreet edges of the main grounds. Work up a sweat and shed some of the restless energy the day had tightened beneath his skin.

Despite the need to continue accommodating the strange demands of their host, he sincerely considered making an escape. Valdez still owed him for that first uncomfortable morning; let him hold things together on his own for a few hours. It was only fair.

But Galin wouldn't abandon him. It was obvious Valdez was every bit as mentally-emotionally-diplomatically exhausted as Galin. More so, perhaps. Valdez had done most of the heavy lifting aboard the lengthy cruise, and he didn't have much natural inclination toward diplomacy.

Dusk had settled into an eerily complete nighttime. Galin stepped from the hovering gangway onto the shore, curious about these new surroundings. They had not returned to the edge of the estate from which they'd departed. This was unfamiliar terrain, rocky and uneven, different from the cultivated architecture and greenery at the edges of the port city. The ground rose steeply ahead, up and up into a high peak. Not a mountain—at least it didn't look like it to the naked eye—but a massive pinnacle just the same.

Barren stone rising jagged against a darkened dome of sky.

Unlike every other spectacle he'd witnessed on Falaris, this marvel possessed no hint of artificial symmetry. This was real. Truly natural. A piece of the moon's original topography jutting from the carefully crafted shore of Lake Laris.

A meandering path had been cut, steep enough to look intimidating. A sturdy stone building stood at the very base of the path, but otherwise Galin had the distinct impression this summit had not been altered in any way.

It was beautiful.

A moment later and Valdez stood at his side, an energetic presence but not quite touching him.

"Well. Fuck," Valdez muttered under his breath, for Galin's ears alone. "Now she's just showing off."

Galin huffed a noiseless laugh and glanced down at his companion. Valdez's face was tilted up, gaze rising high to take in the mammoth height before them. Long hair had begun to escape the high queue at the back of his head, but Valdez didn't seem to notice the strands blowing in his face.

The wiser choice, under normal circumstances, would be to *not* touch. But they were still a mated pair in the eyes of everyone on this lakeshore. And while no one seemed to be paying much attention to them in that moment, Galin found little desire to hold himself back. It was just as inappropriate as ever to take advantage of the situation. But given that Valdez would never know the truth of his feelings, what harm could it do?

He raised a hand to tuck the worst of the escaping wisps behind Valdez's ear. Quick work, and good enough for the moment. Now that they were off the cruise ship and onto solid ground, the wind was significantly less troublesome.

The gesture didn't seem to startle Valdez, but it did earn Galin a smirk and a dart of those strange and expressive eyes meeting his own. Galin dropped his arm back to his side and turned his focus ahead. Away from Valdez. Out across the dark and rocky shore as guest after guest disembarked amid sparse artificial light.

None of the other guests seemed confused at finding themselves at the base of a mysterious peak in the middle of nowhere—a fact that firmly cemented Galin's suspicion that Baell had given everyone else a more complete itinerary. The other guests were all mingling with the distinct air of people who knew what was going on and what was expected of them. Galin tried not to chafe at the unfairness of it. He wouldn't mind some sliver of a clue as to what they were doing here.

Before he could get antsy enough to ask—before even Valdez grew worked up enough to demand answers of anyone nearby—Baell herself approached them, smiling with unabashed humor.

"You gentlemen look a little off balance," she observed, cane tapping lightly on the hard stone path as she stopped directly before them.

"We may have one or two questions," Valdez retorted with just enough fire to signal his impatience. The smile on his face kept his words from crossing into outright rudeness, but even the friendly expression held a sharp edge.

Baell did not appear the faintest bit cowed by Valdez's aggressive attitude. If anything, the smile on her face twisted even brighter. Not with any hint of threat—Galin found no sign of malice in the expression—but with something akin to real amusement.

"Don't worry. I had appropriate attire brought for you, assuming you're interested in participating."

Galin had the distinct feeling he knew what this participation would entail, but he asked anyway. "Appropriate attire for what, exactly?"

"Climbing the summit, of course. Most of your fellow guests will ride the hover-line to the top. Not everyone has the physical capacity for a lengthy hike." She tapped her cane against the stone, a little harder this time, as though to emphasize the point. "You're welcome to join us, of course. The view is well worth it, regardless of your route to the top. But if you should choose to ascend the hard way, I will be waiting to congratulate you."

"You might be waiting a long time," Valdez noted, casting his gaze pointedly up the slope.

Baell chuckled. "Believe me, I am a patient woman. I'm told it can be done in just under four hours if one keeps a vigorous pace."

Whatever constituted a 'vigorous pace,' Galin didn't imagine either himself or Valdez maintaining it all the way up that monstrous path. They both kept up a solid workout regimen aboard ship—Galin required his crew to maintain their health despite the challenges of nearly constant space travel—but this was a far ways beyond the scope of their usual routines.

Yet after several endless hours of physical inactivity, he had energy to burn. Plus they'd eaten aboard the cruise. Galin found he was not inclined to refuse the daunting challenge in Baell's smile.

He gave no visible sign of surprise when Valdez's hand curled around his, twining their fingers together and holding on. He'd grown alarmingly accustomed to such casual intimacies in only a couple short days. But he did turn his head and glance down to find Valdez grinning up at him, eagerness written across that expressive face. Teeth flashed as the grin widened, and Galin raised a single eyebrow in reply.

Valdez leaned deliberately into his side, nudging Galin with an arm. "Come on, old man. What do you say? Race you to the top?"

Galin raised the other eyebrow. Then turned to Baell and said, "Is there somewhere we can change into this 'more appropriate attire?'"

Bell gave an approving nod and turned toward the stone building. "This way, gentlemen."

*

By the time they set foot on the start of the path, they were dressed far more comfortably, though not in any clothing Edda Dak had picked out. Baell had insisted the new outfits were a gift. Thick fabric, almost spongy, soft and well insulated but not overly warm. It had the feel of something engineered for this exact purpose: working and sweating one's way up the side of a miniature mountain, while simultaneously moving into chillier temperatures along the way.

Members of Baell's staff equipped them with climbing boots, walking sticks, canteens. Other tools. It felt like being outfitted for an expedition rather than a recreational hike.

"Necessary for your journey," Baell explained. "We wouldn't want you dehydrating before you reach the summit. And of course, there's no shame in giving up short of completing the climb. There are homing beacons installed in the cuffs of your left sleeves. Activate them, and a private transport unit will collect you and carry you the rest of the way."

Galin kept quiet, but beside him Valdez gave a derisive snort. Cocky, but also familiar in his stubbornness. Of course Valdez would refuse to take what he perceived as the easy way out.

Regardless of Valdez's stubborn pride, Galin sensed that even this was a test. Another chance to prove themselves the tenacious and reliable business partners Baell was seeking.

They would certainly *not* be summoning a shortcut up this peak.

"One last question," Valdez asked before Baell could retreat into the milling crowd of her other guests. "How do we get back down?"

The crowd was significantly smaller than it had been when the party first disembarked the cruise vessel. Dozens of guests had departed completely, boarding quicker transport back to the estate or whatever other business called them. An ambitious few had begun to ascend the mountain on foot, geared up just like Galin and Valdez.

Most of the rest had begun taking turns climbing into small pods—tram cars of sorts—a sizable distance from where the path began. One by one those little carriages, carrying no more than four passengers each, drifted away up the steeper, unclimbable side of the mountain. Purple-tinted lights glowed conspicuously into the timeless and unbroken night. The pods were held aloft in a line, not by struts and cables, but by a controlled magnetic field allowing for a smooth ride.

Beyond them was a barely visible returning line of empty carriages, descending slowly and pausing at the landing to take on passengers before climbing once more.

Baell saw Galin looking and said, "Yes, those are generally the best way back down the mountain. They will continue to run until every last climber finishes their ascent."

Neither Galin nor Valdez spoke as they finally began their journey. The path proved to be less a climb than a steep walk, but it grew quickly challenging. Their steps carried them up a winding path, along what would have been a sheer cliff side if they tried to tackle it head-on. The stone and gravel beneath their feet was a pale, dusty sort of blue, a color that grew darker with every rising step.

Looking upward it was difficult to see anything but more bluish rock.

Silence was a relief after so many hours of perpetual conversation. Galin felt no urge to fill the quiet, and was grateful Valdez seemed equally reluctant. It was a testament to how exhausted Valdez must be that the silence remained unbroken so long. Normally there would be no containing the swirl of energy, of conversation both relevant and chaotic. And normally Galin *would not mind*; he enjoyed listening to Valdez speak.

Sometimes he enjoyed it far more than he should.

But in this moment it felt like a blessing to simply exist. Appreciating the quiet of Valdez matching his pace, falling behind now and then only to rush forward and catch up. The first warm hint of fatigue in his limbs as they continued. Up and up and up. Higher with every forward step.

Somewhere around the two-hour mark, Valdez finally spoke. "I heard some of the other guests talking on the shore. They said this is the tallest natural topography on the entire moon. The engineering team had to design a completely new method of stabilizing the atmospheric dome to accommodate it."

He sounded faintly winded but steady. A match for Galin's own mix of tired but determined energy.

Galin considered this new information for a long moment before answering simply, "Why?"

"Hell if I know." Valdez gave a shrug that Galin caught in his peripheral vision. "It sure as hell would've been simpler to build a dome next to the damn thing. There's more city on the other side of the Shadow Zone—yeah, they actually call it that, I couldn't believe it either—but it would've been a whole lot easier to build around than over."

Galin shook his head. "I doubt 'easy' factors into many of Anatoria Baell's decisions."

Valdez snorted a laugh. "Point. And I'm sure she had some say in the matter, considering she *owns the entire moon*. But aside from dragging her houseguests out here and making them climb to the summit, what's the point of building a dome over a mountain?"

"This is *not* a mountain." Galin let humor trace the edges of the words. He was breathing harder now—the path was beginning to grow even steeper— but the hint of amusement showed through.

"Near enough." Valdez shifted his walking stick into the other hand. "If this doesn't impress her holiness, I don't know what the hell we're going to do. I keep nearly convincing myself she's just stringing us along for her own amusement."

"She's not."

"Yeah, I know," Valdez agreed lightly. "She cornered me on the lake. Didn't say anything useful, but... She can be sincere when she wants to."

Galin bit down a burst of frustration that Valdez hadn't mentioned this before. "Did you make up any more details I should know about?"

Valdez sounded almost hurt when he answered, "Of course not. I wouldn't do that and then not warn you."

Galin didn't *quite* feel guilty for asking, but it was a near thing.

The silence they lapsed into after that was not quite as comfortable as the long moments before. They settled into a rhythm anyway, both of them breathing quick and hard with exertion. Every time Galin considered slowing his pace, Valdez hurried his own, and between the two of them they goaded each other wordlessly up the slope.

The clothing worked well, fabric wicking away the worst of the moisture. Galin still felt winded, sweating hard despite the increasing chill in the air.

His body grew more tired with every step, but it was almost an enjoyable sensation. A well-earned fatigue and a respite from a day—from multiple days—that had been draining in ways he was far less equipped to contend with.

The lack of sunlight stretched around them, perpetual nighttime making it difficult to gauge precisely how long they'd been climbing, but together they reached the summit at last. Exhausted and exhilarated.

The sky that greeted them was stunning and well worth the climb.

It wasn't just starlight scattering across the swathe of night, but an intricate nebula stretching vast and bright above their heads, distorted and faded along the horizon. Pinks and oranges cast diffuse light, spiraling into sultrier shades of purple at the edges. Tendrils swirled together in an elegant arrangement of clouds, the view barely hindered by the transparent dome enclosing the peak. True and devastating beauty.

For several seconds Galin stood at the top of the path—Valdez silent beside him—and simply stared.

"I guess now we know why they built the dome over the mountain," Valdez said in a tone of mystified awe.

Galin did not bother reminding him that it still wasn't a mountain. The main point was unequivocal: with a view like this, no wonder the original surveyors and engineers had decided to burn so many resources enclosing the natural landscape.

He wondered at the timing of their visit. The moon was not a stationary entity, after all. Its quirk of orbit may have left their current location always in the throes of night, but the nebula must come and go. He wondered if Baell had timed her reunion deliberately to guarantee this view for her guests, or if it was a welcome coincidence. He wondered if they would have been invited to climb this path at all for a less staggering view. A starscape would still make for a lovely tableau, but it certainly would not have the fierce impact of cresting the last ridge of stone to see *this*.

He startled when a member of Baell's staff appeared—dressed far too finely for the rustic natural beauty surrounding them—and handed over chilled glasses of water to both Galin and Valdez.

They both drank quickly. Their canteens had run dry about half an hour ago, and the fresh cool water was a reward all its own.

Their empty glasses vanished just as suddenly as the beverages had appeared, and then Galin and Valdez were alone once more.

Well. Not so much alone as momentarily isolated. Left in peace to explore the top of the massive summit. A short distance away was a wide seating area carved directly into the stone, too level to be an amphitheater, but spacious and round and inviting. A couple dozen reunion guests stood and lounged in that vicinity, voices murmuring in a tripping, overlapping chatter that rose and fell on the noisy wind.

Baell sat amid this crowd of extended family.

Her gaze rose just for an instant, taking in the sight of the two men still loitering at a distance. She did not stand, or give any sign of acknowledgment beyond a small nod of her head. A moment later and she returned her attention to her immediate surroundings, tacit dismissal in the way she turned aside.

Galin felt no temptation to join the crowd. He didn't even bother glancing down at Valdez before making his way the opposite direction.

A smaller viewing area stood at a distance, facing out along a rocky vista far below and the span of nebula above. The clear dome arched above them, not nearly as far away as usual. To the left Galin could see the next dome, with its tightly contained life and architecture. To the right the enormous lake that had brought them. But here, in the space that joined the two, he could stare out at the moon's natural landscape stretching endlessly to the horizon.

The sight was extraordinary. As Galin reached the finely-wrought railing that edged the viewing ground, he found himself staring up and up, mesmerized.

Galin Odona was not a young man. He'd seen plenty of wonders, both natural and artificial. He was not easily impressed. Yet the sight before him was among the most beautiful he'd ever witnessed, and for several seconds he held his breath and stared like an awe-struck child.

Beside him, Valdez let out a low breath and a quiet curse, admiration gently packaged in crude syllables. They were words Galin only recognized from hearing Valdez mutter them so many times. Most likely from one of the Earth-based languages he spoke, though given Valdez's background of ships and spaceports, the words could have been picked up anywhere.

"That's a hell of a view," Valdez finally said at a normal volume. Multiple interlocking bars made up the safety railing, intricate despite the thickness of the material. Valdez stepped onto the bottom one like the rung of a ladder—sturdy enough to hold his weight without protest—so that he could cross his arms over the top of the railing. This put him at almost exactly Galin's height as they stared together across the vast expanse.

Galin made no reply. He didn't have to. The view more than spoke for itself.

It felt like an eternity—certainly the longest he'd ever heard Valdez stay quiet without some other physical or mental task to occupy his attention—before either of them spoke.

Of course it was Valdez who broke the silence. His voice was light despite the tired softness of the words. "I hope they don't think we're unromantic for not touching right now. I feel too disgusting to get any closer."

The admission was so blunt and honest, so carelessly frank, that Galin breathed a startled laugh. Affection ignited like a sunburst in his chest, glittering even more brightly than the nebula overhead.

He kept his gaze turned out along the horizon as his face stretched into a foolish, helpless sort of smile. He did not dare look directly at Valdez; too much risk he would see the bright glint in Galin's eyes and recognize the surge of feeling for what it truly was. Galin had kept his secrets—at least this particular secret—for years. He would not risk giving himself away now.

It took him an extra moment to speak, bracing until he could inject wry humor to mask the overabundance of feeling in his voice. "You can have the first shower when we return to the compound." It would be the middle of the night by then. Even though they didn't need to manage their descent on foot, those hovering carriages had not been moving quickly. It might be hours yet before they reached the privacy and respite of their assigned quarters.

"Good," Valdez said with a spark of energy. "I was ready to fight you for it."

Galin made no outward sign of surprise when Baell appeared at his other side. She cast a sideways glance at him by way of greeting.

"Do you like it?" she asked. "The original engineers refused to consider enclosing this peak. So I dismissed the entire team and hired a new one."

Galin hummed a noncommittal sound, too bland to constitute either approval or judgment. He was certainly not *surprised* to hear such a tale, in keeping as it was with everything he knew of Anatoria Baell's character. Exacting, ambitious, unapologetic. In his peripheral vision, he caught sight of the barely discernible tightening in Valdez's shoulders and realized he was struggling not to laugh.

"Ready to go back down?" Baell asked, clearly not offended by the restrained reactions of her guests.

"I suppose we must," Galin agreed, surprised at how reluctant he felt to depart. For all that the hour was already late and his body ached, he found he wasn't ready to go. He didn't imagine he would see another view like this anytime soon.

"Don't worry," Baell reassured with an air of wry humor. "The carriages have transparent roofs, and the view along the direct path is almost as beautiful as this one."

*

When he and Valdez boarded the carriage—a single pod containing only the two of them—Galin saw that Baell was right. The clear carriage roof allowed an unobstructed view, the glittering nebula wide across the night-dark sky.

Tired as he was—tired as they both were—Galin didn't know what to make of the slightly different timbre of silence or the flash of curiosity in Valdez's eyes. There was something considering in that look. A piercing focus that cut beneath the surface in search of something more.

Perhaps he should have recognized the trap.

Valdez could be tactless even when well-rested and under relatively little stress. Especially with those he most trusted—those he knew best—the small but devoted family that made up the *Korria's* crew. All of them were prone to excessive candor, Valdez most of all, and Galin had not been entirely immune over the years. Despite his best efforts to maintain a professional distance, there had been plenty of conversations that veered into personal realms.

Valdez this tired possessed even less sense of propriety than normal, and their current circumstances didn't exactly encourage professional distance.

But Galin *didn't* see it coming. And when Valdez spoke, the first words since boarding their bubble of privacy, Galin nearly startled from his seat at the bluntness of the question.

"Why *haven't* you ever taken a mate?"

Galin stared.

He couldn't decide whether to take offense. It was an invasive question, and surely one Valdez would never ask him in a completely sober frame of mind. But even in the absence of alcohol or other chemicals, 'sober' wasn't exactly the word for either of them in this moment. Galin's own exhaustion hung heavily over his senses, a muddy fog blurring the world around him.

Valdez must certainly have been feeling the same. It didn't seem fair to hold him accountable for the effects when they had both decided together to take on tonight's ambitious climb.

Instead of answering directly, Galin simply said, "Plenty of Remians don't mate or marry."

Valdez gave him the most skeptical look Galin had ever seen, slouching in his seat across the small carriage and peering hard at Galin. Eyes narrowed, lips parted, brows raised.

"Plenty?" Valdez pressed when Galin didn't acknowledge the reaction.

Galin scowled faintly. "Some," he amended. Where he would normally use every tool in his arsenal to shut down such a revealing line of inquiry, he felt more candid than usual. Besides, he was not up to the task of scrounging a true glare or ordering Valdez to let the subject drop.

"You don't have to answer if you don't want," Valdez said, though the stark curiosity remained on his face. "I know it's none of my business. I just wonder... I mean, hell, aside from all the deep space travel? You're a perfect catch. So why not go for it?"

Galin felt an uninvited smile crack through one corner of his scowl. Something wide open and honest in Valdez's tone made it clear the observation wasn't intended as idle flattery. Valdez obviously wasn't interested for his own sake—Galin had never possessed any delusions on that score—but it was surprisingly pleasant to know he saw something appealing enough to make such an observation.

A burst of unaccustomed mischief inspired Galin to ask, "What makes you think it's a deliberate choice?"

Valdez gave him an exasperated look. A stare that conveyed the clear question— *Who do you think you're talking to?*—without saying a word.

"Not to be crude about it," Valdez said when Galin didn't elaborate, "but I do know a couple things about Remian biology."

Galin's brows rose high on his face, and he blinked in surprise. His gaze, wandering a moment before between sky and horizon and his companion, locked hard on Valdez now. It hadn't occurred to him Valdez might know the intricacies of the Remian drive to mate.

Impossible to intuit just how much detail Valdez possessed without delving deeper, but Galin had no such intentions. Clearly it was a complete enough picture to have realized that Galin's age and unmated situation made him statistically improbable.

It wouldn't do to evade the question entirely, so Galin eased back into the cushioned seat—angled his head more comfortably for the view of the sky above—and said, "Biology is not everything." He allowed his gaze to drift farther upward, his vision to blur, and the edges of the nebula turned soft.

"Obviously," Valdez agreed easily. Then, a little bit cautious, a little bit probing, but also entirely sincere, "It's fine if you're not interested in sex."

For the second time tonight, Galin found himself startled into laughter. This burst was louder, a boisterous sound that filled the little hover carriage and snapped Valdez's eyes wider in an instant—wide enough that even in his peripheral vision Galin caught the change in expression. He could feel those eyes drilling into him, curious about his laughter, desperate for information.

Galin kept his focus turned upward and said, in a deliberately light voice, "I have *never* claimed indifference to sex."

Opportunities were few, given his line of work. But contrary to popular misapprehension, Remians weren't averse to casual intimacy. So long as one didn't enjoy such diversions when one's mating drive was in full swing, there was no biological reason to forbear. The rest of the time—without the drive to mate throwing things off kilter and creating the lasting imprint that underpinned a more permanent connection—it was only sex. Simple. Straightforward. Fleeting.

And thoroughly diverting, given a halfway competent partner. Galin may not have had frequent opportunity for such indulgences, but that hardly meant he didn't enjoy them.

He should have left the observation there. He'd already revealed more than he should, and anything further would land far too close to less cautious truths.

Instead his mouth continued as though of its own will, and he listened as if someone else were speaking in his place. "The periodic inconvenience you're wondering about—the biology of the situation—isn't such a hardship. The ordeal is temporary, and it does no lasting harm to simply... *not.*"

Galin was deliberately understating the facts. Every word he'd spoken was true, of course. The mating drive *wasn't* a lengthy or harmful trial.

It was uncomfortable as hell, though. And a challenge every time it happened, to conceal the symptoms from his crew—the agitation and restless energy, the heat like a fever beneath his skin, the preoccupation where he normally did not have any difficulty guarding his thoughts—and even more so to remain aboard ship when he couldn't make arrangements to be elsewhere. It wasn't as though anyone's mating drive followed a consistent cycle.

His own had been growing worse. More frequent. And there was no point pretending he didn't know why.

Before Addison Valdez, Galin had gone nearly a decade without his drive kicking in—an unlikely record for an unmated Remian of his age—and a stretch that lasted the first several years after Addison had joined his crew. Strange and sincere and so different from anyone else Galin had ever known. Slowly as it had overtaken him, he'd been shocked when his own traitorous biology woke him to the fact that he had a problem. His body and heart wanted something he could not have, something close at hand but entirely out of reach. He hadn't considered the expedient choice—sending Addison away—because he refused to punish someone else for his own shortcomings.

But there was little else he could do. His only choice was to maintain his silence and make sure it did not become anyone else's problem.

Valdez had not stopped staring at him. If anything he seemed to be watching even more intently when Galin finally adjusted his posture and tilted his head back down to meet Valdez's eyes. He could see that restless mind turning, turning, turning over the information Galin had already provided and clearly finding it incomplete.

"Okay, but sir... *Why?*"

"Why what, Valdez?"

"Even if you don't want to rearrange your whole life, surely there's someone who wouldn't mind joining you aboard a merchant ship."

"Likely," Galin conceded. "But the point stands. I have no interest in looking for a mate."

Valdez met his eyes, steady and stubborn and brazenly curious. "Did you ever think about it?"

He could say no. Or failing that blatant lie, he could refuse to answer. There were not many people in his present life who knew this particular history. There was no one among his tiny crew. Not because it was truly a secret, but because even after so many years, some things remained too personal.

Which meant he had no explanation for the way he simply *kept talking*. Answering as though Valdez's question were the most reasonable thing in the world.

"A long time ago," he admitted. "When I was a very young man. I had someone. A friend. He made it clear he wanted to be more, and I very much wanted the same."

Valdez leaned forward in his seat and braced his elbows on his knees, clasped his hands tightly together. "What happened?"

"He died." Galin's chest tightened with a lingering shadow of loss. Seventy years was a long time, but some things never faded completely.

"*Fuck*," Valdez breathed. "I'm so sorry."

"Thank you." Galin let his gaze drift to the side, out along the stony slope. "It was a stupid accident that took him. Malfunctioning safety equipment. When my mating drive began less than a week later I thought the universe was playing some sort of sick prank on me. It was..." *Awful*, he thought, but didn't say the word out loud because it wasn't enough. It didn't convey just how empty and desperate and frantic he had felt, in those days of heartache running up against a physical need worse than anything he'd ever experienced.

He'd resisted that first drive; he had not once regretted the decision.

"And since then?" The question sounded lost and a little bit sad. As though even though Galin hadn't spoken the worst of his memories aloud, Valdez was intuiting them anyway, insightful but helpless to offer comfort.

Galin did not require comfort. He was well accustomed to these feelings. They'd been with him a very long time.

He kept his head turned aside, ignoring the weight of Valdez's watchful focus in order to continue, "There wasn't anyone else. At the time, or after. I considered looking, but it never... When my time came again, I simply wasn't interested. Years had passed."

Nearly a decade, in fact. Long enough he'd begun to wonder if the drive to mate would ever return to him at all. "I was no longer grieving. But I had no intention of taking a mate or marrying—of upending my life and fitting someone else into it—just for the sake of biological convenience."

Valdez remained silent, mulling the words through.

Galin felt compelled to explain. "Plenty of Remians make a different choice. I've witnessed profound bonds grow from connections of convenience. The mating imprint can be a powerful beginning. But for me... I didn't see the point. And the more years passed, the more certain I became that I'm better off alone."

He'd never been truly alone. There had always been his family, even when he let far too much time pass between visits and communiqués. And of course his crew, a family of a different sort. His to protect. He hadn't ever repented his decision enough to pursue a different course.

He certainly hadn't intended to lose all his better sense over someone he could not have.

"So you've never seriously considered it since?" Valdez asked in an uncharacteristically soft voice. Not hesitant exactly, but cautious in his curiosity. "All these years, and you've never wanted *anyone else*?"

Galin froze.

The question hung in the air between them. There was nothing accusatory in either Valdez's words or tone. How could there be when he had no idea how entirely wrong he was? But the question lodged like an accusation in Galin's chest anyway. Damning. Because of course Galin had thought about it since. Had *wanted someone* since.

He could not very well admit this to Valdez. Bad enough the thoughts were there in his head. He had no intention of confessing that, more recently, when his mind wandered to thoughts of taking a mate, it was Valdez himself who occupied every idle fantasy.

Ridiculous to imagine Valdez could want him. Even more ridiculous to imagine Valdez staying by his side for the rest of their mutual lives.

Galin had never been tempted to confess these truths to anyone. He was the captain. The boss. He had responsibilities to the people in his employ, and a code of conduct that served him well. No good could come of putting someone in the untenable position of needing to reject his unwanted advances. Galin had complete confidence Valdez would speak his mind if put in such a situation, but that didn't make it right.

It wasn't usually difficult, keeping things to himself. Galin did not have to lie in order to guard these feelings. That they'd grown more potent instead of waning was a challenge, but a surmountable one. Galin cared for every member of his crew, as both their captain and their friend. Add to that connection the simple fact that the *Korria* ran better with Valdez aboard, and Galin would have to be several varieties of fool to speak this particular truth. All the more so given the way their stay on Falaris had blurred the boundaries of propriety between them.

But he also did not dare lie outright. Valdez knew him too well—knew just how terrible a liar he was— knew every twitch and tell that might give him away. Better to not speak at all than to try and lie to Valdez's face.

Even silence would be damning if Valdez's quick mind caught up with him, so Galin belatedly answered, "I didn't say that. 'Never' is a long time. Of course I've wanted. But in the end, I've never chosen to pursue anyone."

"Why not?" Valdez pressed, oblivious to Galin's reticence.

"For reasons that are entirely personal and *none of your concern*," Galin answered sternly. He was suddenly, sharply aware of just how much he had already revealed. Fatigue was no excuse. Where the hell had his sense of caution gone? Addison Valdez was far too clever to trust with so many pieces of this puzzle.

"But sir!" Valdez protested, rather than dropping the subject immediately.

"Enough," Galin said in the same cutting tone. It was the voice that shut down arguments among his crew, the voice that ended negotiations. "This conversation is closed. And I would appreciate if it remained that way for the foreseeable future." He did not want to revisit these confidences.

He did not dare.

*

By the time they reached their rooms, Galin was far too drowsy to remain on edge. They both were. All conversation between them had petered out before they even disembarked the carriage and had not resumed through the entire hover-lift ride back to Baell's estate.

Galin kept his word and allowed Valdez the first shower, busying himself in an effort to remain upright for his own turn. He checked in with the ship despite the late hour and reassured himself that all was well there. Rielle sounded sleepy and just shy of homicidal at being woken, but she gave him a quick update of all the nothing that had happened in his absence. He heard Keeth rouse in the background—a faint *Gamina?* answered by a *Shush, go back to sleep*—but when Rielle signed off, she managed to do it without so much as a snarl.

By the time the comm line cut, the washroom door was open. Valdez emerged already dressed in the same soft sleeping clothes he favored aboard ship. Baggy pants, bare feet. A shirt with short sleeves and a neckline that had stretched too wide over the years.

All of it far more casual than their surroundings, and yet Valdez looked completely at ease.

"All yours," came the sleepy murmur as he passed Galin toward the bed. Even those two words sounded bleary with exhaustion. It had been a damnably long day.

When Galin emerged from the washroom dressed for sleep himself, Valdez had already burrowed beneath the covers on the far side of the enormous bed. He lay sprawled carelessly on his back, head turned to the side and face half-squashed into the pillow. His hair was still wet enough to dampen the fabric.

His eyes were closed. His chest rose and fell steadily.

Galin knew he should dim the lights and go to sleep himself. He should certainly not stand here staring like a smitten fool. But for several long seconds he couldn't help it. Valdez looked so relaxed, so loose and calm and *quiet.* There was unaccustomed stillness in him; it hardly seemed possible this was the same frenetic young man who filled the *Korria* with such overabundant energy.

He was beautiful. Galin's chest hurt looking at him.

*It's not fair,* he thought in a burst of idle frustration. Not because his feelings weren't returned—he was not a man inclined toward pretty delusions—but because the ache behind his ribs was overwhelming. He knew what this was. Knew what to call it. He knew there was no one he could trust with a secret so solitary, and that was *fine*.

But it also was not fair: being in love shouldn't hurt this much.

He tore his gaze from Valdez with difficulty and shifted his weight, looking instead at the carefully folded pile of blankets at the foot of the bed. Another moment and his gaze dropped further, through the door and toward the open floor of the sitting room beyond.

A scowl twisted his mouth at the corners. For reasons entirely practical, he did not look forward to sleeping on the hard floor tonight. His physical body ached almost as much as his heart after the day's exertions. Even if he slept in an actual bed, he would likely wake to significant discomfort. Sleeping on the ground would exacerbate the problem, and just the thought made his head throb dully.

But he couldn't wake Valdez and demand they switch places. That would be both selfish and unkind, and he would not do it.

He glanced to the bed again, and there was longing in his gaze. Not for the bed's occupant this time, but for the soft mattress and abundance of pillows. Perhaps he could compromise: wake Valdez and ask to share after all. It would look strange after the fuss Galin had made the past two nights; Valdez would almost certainly wonder why tonight was different. And Galin couldn't exactly explain that tonight physical exhaustion was outweighing his better sense.

No. He would have to take the floor. Even if he could bear to wake Valdez when he looked so peaceful, he could think of *nothing to say*.

"For fuck's sake," Valdez growled without opening his eyes. "Get over here already. There's plenty of room."

Galin's attention snapped sharply back to the bed's sole occupant. Valdez's eyes were open, peering up at him in blatant challenge.

"I..." He still did not know what to say. It seemed wrong to simply agree, but he couldn't bring himself to argue or refuse. Instead he simply stood there gawping, caught between responses and unable to answer at all.

Valdez's eyes narrowed and he propped himself up on his elbows. "Okay, seriously. *Why?* Why is this such a big deal?"

Galin couldn't answer.

Eventually Valdez dropped onto his back, obviously tired of waiting. Another moment, a frustrated huff of breath, and he turned onto his side. Putting his back to Galin and tugging the blankets over his shoulder. Even in the absence of other evidence, the tense line of his back would have been enough to convey frustration, perhaps even a shadow of hurt. Galin swallowed a pulse of guilt at the thought.

He breathed a barely audible sigh.

A quick touch of the control panel dimmed the lights, leaving the room in near-total darkness. Galin navigated carefully across the narrow aisle, finding the edge of the bed and easing beneath the covers. The sheets were cool, but they warmed quickly. The pillow squashed pleasantly beneath his head, and he settled onto his back. For only a moment, he lay there blinking heavily in the silence.

Then, quick and smooth and steady, Galin fell asleep.

# Chapter Nine

Addison woke, warm and slow, and even better rested than the day before.

His mind was reluctant to claw up from pleasant but insubstantial dreams. A dull ache ran the entire length of his body, and there was stiffness in his limbs. Light nudged at his closed eyelids, though not nearly the same sharp brightness that had woken him the morning before.

He shifted, a prelude to a stretch, but froze when the rest of his senses roused and caught up with his surroundings.

There were arms wrapped loosely around him, holding him close. He was pressed tightly to his captain's broad chest, curling into Odona's heat as though he had any right to be here. His head tucked beneath Odona's jaw, and steady breath feathered Addison's sleep-static hair.

A slow, even pulse beat beneath his palm where Addison's hand pressed between them. Odona's heart was positioned lower in his chest than a Human heart, but it followed a familiar rhythm.

Addison held his breath as all of this registered. He was entirely awake now, and his own pulse raced faster. His gaze darted to take in more information, even as the rest of him held perfectly still. It was obvious enough what had happened. Despite the enormous sprawl of the bed between them, they'd moved together during the night. Perfectly predictable.

Less likely was the fact that they hadn't met in the middle. They were near the edge—Odona's side of the bed—which meant Addison had encroached all the way across the mattress last night and into Odona's space. All without waking. All without noticing the strangeness of the situation.

He needed to extricate himself. Simple. He could deal with the fact that Odona might wake at the movement. It would be awkward, but nothing they couldn't set aside, maybe even laugh over when they were finally able to return to their work and their normal life.

Addison had no explanation for the way he remained exactly where he was instead. He could try to rationalize that it was still early, they'd gotten back impossibly late last night, he'd never seen Odona so exhausted. Surely it was better to let him sleep. No harm lying quiet and patient in the meantime, wondering why this inadvertent intimacy felt so damn comfortable.

The problem was, he didn't just feel comfortable: he felt good. It was far too easy to linger in the protective circle of Odona's arms.

His mind wandered in the quiet. Wakefulness brought back the surreal quality of last night's conversation, the unaccustomed candor during their ride down the mountain. Now, recovered from the physical and mental exhaustion of a draining day, Addison was appalled at himself for asking such personal questions. Odona had never been one to confide his private life, no matter how close he seemed with the *Korria's* small crew; but he had confided last night. A barrage of intrusive interrogations, and Odona had answered—had kept answering—painting a picture Addison had never considered before.

Sometimes he managed to forget that Odona was more than a century old. That was a lot of years—a lot of *life*—a lot of time to experience change and loss and more.

It was also a long time to be alone, for a man who wasn't designed for solitude.

Addison didn't think he was jumping to the wrong conclusion here. Yes, there were plenty of people who preferred a life free of romantic attachments. He'd known his share of them. Addison had always considered Odona among them, from the way he put ship and crew above all else.

But now he found himself reevaluating. Despite the newness of this glimpse into intensely personal realms, Addison knew Odona well enough to read between the lines. Practicality had kept him alone so far, but there was no mistaking the simple fact: Odona was a romantic at heart. And he was lonely.

Not just lonely, Addison considered with a confusing wave of feeling. There was someone specific. Someone Odona wanted and couldn't have. The sentiment had been subtle but undeniable in the way he'd evaded Addison's final questions on the mountain. Answering without really answering. Abruptly setting aside the candor that had goaded Addison forward in the first place.

*Of course I've wanted*, Odona had said. And, *Never is a long time*.

And then a shutdown so complete it left Addison's head spinning. A stern and impenetrable wall had risen between them. The sudden change only made sense if Odona had something to hide.

There were only so many possible suspects. If Odona were pining for some friend or colleague Addison didn't know, there would be no reason for defensiveness. Which left their tiny crew. Laia Keeth, Gamina Rielle, Edda Dak. All of them simultaneously ridiculous to consider, and yet stunningly plausible. Obviously a good captain infatuated with a member of his crew would go to great lengths to make sure nobody suspected. The potential for awkwardness, for rejection, for disruption to the running of their business...

Not to mention the fact that Galin Odona was a *good man*. One who would never risk hurting someone close to him.

It could be Laia or Gamina, but the more Addison considered the possibility, the more certain he was that neither woman was the source of Odona's consternation. Difficult as it might be to harbor feelings for a woman who was both mated and married, surely the ship wouldn't shake apart if anyone suspected.

He did not spare even a fleeting what-if for the possibility that it might be him. Closely as they worked, and terrible as the man was at dissembling, it was impossible to imagine Odona successfully hiding such an infatuation.

That left Edda Dak. Youngest member of the crew—though he barely beat Addison out for the title—and a jarringly plausible candidate. Edda was a smart young man. Smooth and clever. He carried himself with a confidence far beyond his years. It was obvious just looking at him that he sat easier in his skin than Addison ever had or would. Edda was infuriatingly handsome too, with his perpetual dry smile, scattered freckles, curly hair.

Hell, Addison had entertained a fantasy or two himself. He couldn't blame Odona for noticing Edda was damned easy to look at. He sure as hell shouldn't be miffed about it.

He *wasn't* miffed. The feeling buzzing beneath his skin wasn't anything like anger. But it was *something*, sullen and achy and unpleasant. Imagining Odona with Edda Dak—imagining Odona with *anyone*—

kindled a white-hot ember of denial in the pit of Addison's stomach.

It *hurt.*

It shouldn't hurt. Addison had no reason to disapprove, especially of something that would never happen. Odona sure as hell wasn't going to admit the truth. He hadn't admitted it even to Addison, for all that the conclusion was there in plain sight. There was no excuse for the burst of displeasure in Addison's chest.

He had no damn right to be jealous.

Just like he had no damn right to enjoy being held warm and secure in Odona's arms.

Fuck.

Addison took slow, deliberate care not to wake his captain when he finally untangled himself and returned to his own side of the bed. His efforts were successful. He detected no change in Odona's breathing, no tensing surprise, no flicker of motion beneath closed eyelids. When he reached his own pillow, he simply lay there for a long time, staring at the ceiling.

He was not good at self-delusion. Now that he understood just how much he enjoyed Odona touching him, he could not simply set the knowledge aside. He couldn't tell himself he *didn't* want Odona to touch him in even more intimate ways. And that?

That was a problem.

But maybe it was a temporary problem.

Hell, of course he was preoccupied with Odona. These last couple days had been one long mind game. All the mental gymnastics of a lengthy con as they put forward a united front of public intimacy. He'd never occupied anyone's personal space quite so thoroughly as he had Odona's since arriving on Falaris. He'd always been attracted to Odona—nothing new there— but this was different. This was no idle appreciation; this was *more*. After too many hours in close proximity, Addison needed out.

No. Not just out. He needed a distraction.

Somewhere to redirect his energies. Someone uncomplicated, to engage in more honest intimacies. This damn moon was a major point of commerce within the solar system. There were bound to be drinking and social establishments of every conceivable variety in the city that abutted the estate. Addison could make a new acquaintance—find someone tall and broad and easy to look at—someone interested in going somewhere more private.

Someone who wanted to fuck and then go their separate ways.

Easy, straightforward, satisfying. Potentially tricky considering the consequences if Baell were to find out, but he would be careful. He just needed to find the right establishment, discreet and out of the way, and make a connection.

He wouldn't be able to duck out during the day. He'd already left Odona in the lurch once, and that was one time too many; he had no intention of doing it again. He would have to tough it out through brunch and mingling and whatever else Baell had planned for the afternoon. Stick close to Odona's side without letting on just how much he enjoyed being there. Keep the guilty twinge—the feeling of taking advantage of an unwelcome situation *he had created*—from showing on his face every time he leaned in close and took Odona's hand.

Later tonight he could slip away. After dinner things would quiet down, guests would meander about their private business, and Addison could escape unnoticed for a while.

Decision made, he pushed himself upright and slid his legs over the edge of the bed. It was still early, but he wasn't likely to get any further sleep.

He would find someone tonight. And then he would return before morning.

Odona never needed to know there was a problem.

*Chapter Ten*

Galin could not account for the subtle shift in Valdez's behavior as they joined the crowd of guests for a late breakfast. There was something surreptitious in the way Valdez dropped his gaze every time their eyes met. A ridiculous thing to worry over when Valdez was as bold as ever about occupying his personal space—about touching him in all the ways they had grown so improbably accustomed to—but it lodged a kernel of uncertainty in Galin's chest just the same.

He didn't think their conversation last night had contained enough of the truth to make Valdez uncomfortable. Galin still couldn't believe how openly he'd allowed himself to discuss such intensely personal matters. But for all that he'd been completely exhausted, he remained confident he hadn't given away his most vital secret.

Even if he doubted his own judgment, he had one nearly indisputable piece of evidence: Valdez had insisted on sharing the bed with him last night. Surely he would not have pushed the issue if he'd assembled the pieces into a coherent whole and recognized Galin's less-than-professional interest.

That Valdez had woken and begun the day long before Galin was not a troubling fact. Hell, Valdez always preferred an early start to the day, even when 'day' was an artificially imposed construct of the *Korria's* ship-board computer.

But the fact remained. Valdez was behaving differently today. Not just through breakfast, but during the parade of additional social activities: the absolute joke of half-hearted sporting events on the lawn of the main courtyard; the late afternoon meal; the tour of complicated gardens that sprawled across several rooftops at the opposite end of the estate. The weather held beautiful throughout, artificial as it was, and Valdez remained at Galin's side almost constantly.

But he was quiet—no normal state of affairs— and Galin didn't know what to make of it.

He couldn't very well ask. Aside from the fact that they were never alone among the crowd, what was he supposed to say? *You're not talking enough. I'm sorry if I made you uncomfortable with my personal business last night. Would it help if I took some of it back?*

There was no taking it back. The information was already out, and it wasn't even all that damning.

Galin caught Baell's eye a handful of times during the seemingly endless day. He didn't know what to make of the look she gave him, measurably less severe than before, but nowhere near decisively approving. It was maddening to still be trapped in limbo, wondering if their presence here was accomplishing anything at all.

Despite how closely attuned he was to Valdez's presence, Galin didn't notice immediately when he disappeared.

It was well after the dinner hour, nightfall deepening and many of the other guests beginning to disperse. Late enough that Galin himself had begun the mental calculations of how best to escape for the night. With only one more day of this nonsense ahead of them, he was eager to speed things along.

It wasn't unusual for Valdez to excuse himself for brief intervals. Yes, they mostly stuck close together, but there was no need to remain constantly within each other's line of sight. There were plenty of reasons to vanish from time to time. Strategy, personal necessity, a simple moment of calm away from prying eyes.

With the sole exception of Valdez's sleep-deprived tantrum on their first day here, these interludes were always short. A brief respite, and then back into the fray, side-by-side. They had a job to do, and only one chance to do it right. But when half an hour passed and Valdez didn't return, Galin began to wonder if he'd missed something.

He allowed until the turn of the hour, just in case, before excusing himself from the most recent cluster of conversation that had closed in around him. Fatigue dragged at him as he traveled the short journey back to their assigned rooms. This was a different weight of tiredness from the night before.

His body felt well rested after a sound night's sleep, and the lingering ache in his limbs had faded over the course of the day. But he craved quiet and privacy, and he had not truly experienced either of those things since reaching Falaris.

He would be glad when this bizarre engagement was over, whatever the outcome.

When he reached Ruke Hall there was no sign of Valdez. Their room stood empty, freshly cleaned in their absence. It was impossible to tell if Valdez had been here recently, but clearly he was elsewhere now.

Confusion, rather than worry, compelled Galin to take out his personal comm link. The scale tipped closer to concern when his efforts to transmit a signal were met with the quiet, sullen beep that meant Valdez's comm had been turned deliberately off.

He couldn't imagine Valdez finding trouble in so short a time, but he also couldn't shake the strangeness of his absence. For Valdez to leave without giving any indication of where he intended to go or when he might be back? Improbable.

Galin considered for a moment, trying to decide how ridiculous he would feel, then finally contacted the ship. Laia Keeth answered, but when Galin asked if Valdez had come aboard, her answer was immediate and perplexed.

"No, sir. Is everything all right?"

"Yes." It wasn't entirely a lie. Galin knew full well he was being foolish. Valdez had been gone barely an hour, and Baell's estate was situated in one of the safest cities in the quadrant. Even if Valdez had left the grounds, it wasn't as though they were prisoners here. They were both allowed to leave at any time. "Will you do me a favor and track his comm location?"

"Are you sure everything's all right?" Keeth pressed.

"We lost track of each other, and I can't reach him. He's probably close by. I just need to know where to look."

Ridiculous. But he would worry about that later. *After* finding his wayward employee and making certain nothing had gone wrong.

"I've got his coordinates," Keeth reported after several seconds of silence. "I can give you the name of the establishment and the closest intersection."

"Thank you." Galin turned back for the hall. Foolish or not, he wouldn't rest easy until he saw Valdez with his own eyes.

*

The location Keeth provided took him through the city, all the way to the space port at the farthest edge. It was a quick enough journey for the craft and driver Galin borrowed from Baell's garage. He would have preferred to navigate the small vehicle himself— he didn't much like being chauffeured—but his initial protests had been soundly shot down.

He knew better than to push when he stood on unfamiliar ground.

"How long will you be?" his driver asked once they were stationary. The question carried a practiced mix of deference and impatience.

"You don't need to wait," Galin answered without hesitation. "If I'm not back in ten minutes, you can return to the estate without me." There were other transport options, especially this close to the main port. There were plenty of transit services, both public and private, and Galin could always call the compound and request another driver. Hell, his own vessel was docked in the vicinity if for some reason he couldn't retrace his steps.

He might be in and out of this place quickly enough to simply ride directly back to the estate grounds; but the last thing he wanted was to go inside knowing someone would be waiting for him the entire time.

The building was a low-to-the-ground, decrepit looking dive. Understated, seedier than the surrounding hostels and restaurants. The block was well lit and clean enough, which meant the aura of disrepair around this particular establishment had an almost deliberate feel to it. An ambiance catering to a less selective clientele than some of the snootier lounges up the block.

Large double doors swung frequently open beneath a sign missing so many letters as to be illegible. There were no windows. But at least a steady stream of people came and went before his eyes. Laughing faces, friendly bodies leaning on each other, arms around waists and shoulders. Ragged as the building might look, it also raised none of his hackles. It was the sort of place he might willingly go for a drink under normal circumstances.

He stepped onto the curb and braced himself before pushing through the busy crowd.

Immediately inside the double doors, he came to an abrupt halt, startled at the scope of the space before him. Part dimly lit bar, part colorful club, *all* noisy and chaotic. It seemed impossible for all of this to exist under the compact roof he had glimpsed from the street. One enormous room spread out before him, a space set up to look even larger thanks to mirrors on every conceivable surface—even the ceiling.

The rough-edged aura from the outside of the building was somehow softer inside, though the walls and bannisters and even the bar he could glimpse through the throngs all had a similar rustic feel. The dim lighting created a contradictory sense of intimacy alongside an absolute cacophony of conversation and music.

The doors he'd just stepped through opened at the top of a shallow flight of stairs, wide enough for at least twenty people to descend simultaneously arm-in-arm. Galin hesitated at the top, taking it all in. His gaze wandered down across a restless and radiant sea of moving bodies.

Most of the club's patrons were dancing to music that thumped such a deep rhythm Galin could feel it in his chest. Partners and groups twisted together, rowdy and energetic, filling the sprawling dance floor. The bar stretched across one wall, and a haphazard forest of bottles and barrels and crates made for an impressive miniature mountain range behind it.

Galin considered the possibility that Valdez could be on the dance floor, but he quickly dismissed the notion. Not because it was truly unlikely, but because if that *was* Valdez's current location, Galin had no hope of finding him. He made for the darker area near the bar instead, weaving down the stairs between dozens of people who all shoved and hurried like they were on urgent missions of their own.

Away from the brighter lights of the dance floor, Galin moved with steady purpose. There was enough illumination to navigate easily between tables, but everything had a blueish tinge that made it difficult to focus. Galin brushed off multiple greetings and propositions as he made his way through clusters of people. This crowd was nowhere near as thick as the one he'd seen dancing, but maneuvering through without stepping on toes or knocking into anyone still presented a challenge.

At last he spotted Valdez at a tall, heavily shadowed table near the farthest end of the bar.

The shadows weren't quite heavy enough to conceal his face—once in range Galin spotted him easily—or to hide his easy slouch. Valdez sat on a tall stool, grinning wickedly and half leaning on the empty table beside him. He held a small bottle of some beverage that glowed faintly blue. Whatever the drink was, he hadn't consumed much of it.

He also wasn't alone.

Fury rose beneath Galin's skin, as immediate as it was irrational, a twisting and unpleasant sensation that hurried his pulse and turned his breath shallow. The companion standing beside Valdez's table was broad and handsome, and even from halfway across the room Galin could see just how little space separated the two men.

Jealousy snapped inside him, a sharp-edged and ugly thing. Galin put it aside. He had no standing to be territorial, regardless of the contours of their ruse.

His feelings for Valdez were no more justifiable now than they'd been before this strange charade. The fact that Valdez was to blame for their predicament did not give Galin grounds for the possessive instincts threatening to overwhelm him. Bad enough he kept catching himself enjoying their unaccustomed proximity, the nearly constant physical contact, the casual way Valdez touched him like only a mate should.

But. Damn it.

This wasn't only about Galin and the things he had no standing to want. There were more tangible reasons Valdez should not be here—should not be receptive to a stranger's advances—should not be so obviously flirting in public. With so much at stake, they couldn't afford to be careless. And this? This was unforgivably careless.

Falaris was not a large port of call, and Baell's guests were clearly not restricted to the estate. Unlikely as it was that any of them would come *here*, the wrong witness could destroy any hope the *Korria* might have of winning over their skittish host. Valdez's ill-timed venture could cost them the contract.

Galin would not stand by and let their efforts crumble to nothing.

Shoving his more complicated emotions aside, he took firm hold of blunt and simple anger. He embraced a more detached disbelief at Valdez's recklessness, at the obvious and willful lack of reasonable judgment.

Then, with a single rigid step, Galin started forward.

*Chapter Eleven*

Addison's laughter cut short when his new companion crowded the rest of the way into his space and kissed him.

A warm hand curled at his jaw, and he obeyed the wordless guidance. He tilted his head farther back, angling his body to better welcome the broad wall of muscle pressing close.

Bann was D'Arveshe, which meant he was big, sturdy, and ran hot to the touch. He felt damn good. Even better when he turned Addison on the tall stool and slipped between his legs, maneuvering with all the bluntness of a man who had done this plenty of times before.

Fantastic. Addison had no problem with inexperienced partners, but tonight? Tonight he wanted someone to come at him with confidence— someone to take him completely apart and wipe all his other distractions away.

This was a perfect start. It was an excellent kiss, and when it ended Bann didn't retreat from Addison's space.

"I like you," Bann said. "I think I'd like you even more somewhere private. I could show you my place."

Addison grinned, all teeth. "Are you going to make it worth my while? I'm a busy man."

Bann's startled laugh was throaty and warm with delight. "Oh, you are *cocky*. I'm going to enjoy taking you to pieces."

Addison only grinned wider and made a show of turning away, reaching for his drink without making any effort whatsoever to escape the promising invasion of his personal space. Bann's fingers slipped through the loose strands of his hair, suggestive and patient, and *oh*. Addison had a *very good feeling* about how tonight was about to go.

Familiar movement caught at the edge of Addison's vision, and he raised his eyes—froze with the drink halfway to his mouth when he realized why he recognized that storming gait.

Odona wore a thunderous expression to match his pace, and there was heavy displeasure in his approach. He was still several steps away when Bann belatedly turned to follow Addison's line of sight. A huff of breath cut through the intimate space between them, signaling that Bann had caught sight of the impending torrent bearing down on them.

Confused incredulity tinged Bann's words when he muttered, "What in the holy name of—" But he cut himself short, perhaps wisely, when Odona reached their table and simply *stopped*.

For several godawful seconds, nobody spoke. Fuck, Addison had *not* anticipated an interruption. He'd picked this location specifically for its dusty anonymity and distance from the estate—it was exactly the sort of place where he couldn't imagine any of Baell's guests setting foot—and he sure as hell hadn't expected Odona would be concerned enough to follow him.

Through the irritation, Addison felt a twinge of self-inflicted frustration. Much as he'd hoped to keep his plans tonight private, he should have warned Odona he was leaving. At minimum he should've left a note in their shared rooms. Vanishing without any explanation after days joined at the hip... He should damn well have guessed the strategy wouldn't fly.

His lapse didn't explain the intensity of the anger on Odona's face, though.

It was Odona who broke the straining tension, locking his eyes on Addison's companion and speaking in a voice of thinly contained wrath. "Leave."

Bann straightened and eased out of Addison's space, but he didn't retreat. "Who are you?"

Odona's eyes narrowed and he rounded the table to close the remaining distance. Addison watched him, torn between irritation and something more like awe. He'd never seen Odona throw a punch, and he was reasonably sure there would be no fisticuffs now; but there was purpose in Odona's stride, and a rigid set to his shoulders. Addison couldn't entirely rule out the possibility.

He found himself bracing for the worst as the two men faced off directly in front of him. A wordless contest to see who could look more intimidating.

Odona loomed a couple inches taller than Addison's new friend, but it was clear Bann had no intention of backing down.

"I will only repeat myself this once," Odona said, instead of answering the question. "*Leave*."

Bann sneered, and the expression bared exceptionally sharp canines. "I don't think so. If he wanted what you're offering, he wouldn't be here in the first place."

Odona's eyes narrowed even further, into pitch black slits of potent feeling. Addison knew he had to put a stop to this. Odona was probably bluffing—not really looking for a fight—but Bann? Bann might start swinging if this confrontation escalated. Addison didn't really know him well enough to be sure, and a fight was the last damn thing they needed.

"Enough." He slumped on his high stool, bracing one elbow on the table. Both men stared at him hard, gazes locking on like tractor beams. Addison looked Bann directly in the eye. "Hey. So. I know this is awkward. But you should probably go."

Bann gawped at him, incredulous and obviously offended. "You can't be serious. This jerk shows up and starts barking orders like he owns the place, and you tell *me* to walk? We were just getting to know each other."

"Yeah." Addison let disappointed warmth infuse the word. "Look, I don't want you to think... This isn't about you, okay? I'm sure you'll find someone to salvage your night."

Bann's expression softened, and he turned to face Addison directly. Effectively breaking the standoff. There was something deliberate in the way he cut Odona out of the discussion without turning his back completely. The look he gave Addison felt suspiciously like worry.

"You sure, kid?" The question was pitched low. Private—not so quiet Odona wouldn't hear—but intimate and careful. "I can stick around. We don't have to go anywhere."

And oh, that offer was genuinely kind. There was no more suggestion of casual intimacy in Bann's tone or demeanor. This was pure concern, because Odona was doing a damn good impression of a jealous boyfriend. Bann had no way to know there was no danger. That Odona wasn't his boyfriend, let alone the jealous type, and *certainly* not prone to violence. Or that Addison wasn't—had *never once* been—scared of the man looming so ominously before him.

He let his own expression soften, ignoring the weight of Odona's glare. He met Bann's look with a careful smile and gave his massive arm a reassuring squeeze.

"I'm fine," he said. "Truly. But thank you."

Bann peered at him for a long moment. Peered *through him*, as though trying to gauge his sincerity. It seemed like an eternity before the shrug and retreat that followed, as Bann removed himself from between Addison and Odona. A small nod was all the goodbye he offered before disappearing into the crowd.

Addison watched Bann go with a wistful sort of regret. His skin felt too tight, his whole body primed for the kind of activity he was clearly not going to indulge in tonight after all. Bann had been the perfect answer to Addison's misguided cravings, and he was *walking away.* Leaving Addison alone with his glowering captain. Leaving him riled and unsatisfied and just as off-balance as he'd been when he first walked through those doors.

He embraced his own nova-burst of irritation. Anger was still a better strategic choice than the messy new desires he'd woken up considering this morning. Anger was easier, and Addison clung to it as he spun on his stool in order to look Odona directly in the face. A scowl twisted his own expression, and for a long moment they simply stared at each other. Addison's back pressed to the edge of the table, and he braced his elbows atop the smooth surface, slouching like a petulant child.

Fuck it, who needed dignity when he was this pissed off?

Odona still hadn't spoken, so finally Addison snapped, "You planning to explain what the *fuck* that was?"

The anger in Odona's eyes flashed brighter, and he took a single step forward. Closer. Standing near enough to touch now, not that Addison would have dared. It took visible effort for him to unclench his jaw and speak, only to evade Addison's question in favor of asking his own.

"What the hell do you think you're doing here tonight?"

Addison scowled harder. "I think it's pretty obvious what I was *trying* to do here tonight." He considered standing up and squaring off, posturing for a fight even though there was no universe in which Odona would meet him with violence. But dismounting his stool would make their height disparity even more apparent. Odona already had plenty of advantage on that score; Addison wasn't about to give him even more of one.

"Why would you think this is acceptable?" Odona demanded.

Being at the center of his complete focus was overwhelming. Addison could count on one hand the number of times he'd held Odona's attention so completely. And even though most of them had occurred during impassioned arguments, there was something about *this time* that made his skin heat and his pulse speed. Maybe he could blame Bann's departure and the fact that he no longer had any hope of outside satisfaction tonight. That seemed a reasonable possibility.

Reasonable enough that Addison straightened from his slouch and demanded, "Since when is it any of your business who I fuck?"

Even in the heavy shadows swathing this section of the club, the flush that spread across Odona's face was nearly as pronounced as the widening of all-black eyes. It didn't look like anger. Surprise, certainly, with some other indecipherable mix of feelings alongside. But Addison knew Odona well enough to recognize the fact that—just for an instant—the fury had vanished completely.

It returned a moment later, accompanied by a deep crease at the very center of Odona's brow. "It's my business so long as we're on this damn moon, since *you* told a potential employer that you are my mate!"

Oh. Fuck. The way Odona raised his voice should *not* have kindled this particular kind of warmth in Addison's chest. He bit the inside of his cheek and held back an even angrier retort.

Odona seemed to struggle with himself for a moment, and then in a softer voice said, "If anyone were to see you—"

"They won't," Addison interrupted. "I chose this place for a reason."

He didn't need to cast his gaze around them to make sure his point would land. He'd chosen this club as much for the crowd and noise as for its proximity to the main port. There was anonymity in such a swarming space. Insulation in both physical distance from Baell's compound and the rundown appearance of the place. The establishment was filled to capacity from the edges of the dance floor to the comparable quiet—still not quiet at all—of the corner he had staked out for himself.

No one should have noticed him here. Certainly Odona shouldn't have spotted him so easily, even if he'd been following the tracking information in Addison's comm link. But here Odona stood regardless, having picked him out of the crowd with unlikely ease, and Addison knew what the retort would be even before Odona spoke.

"*I* found you, didn't I? Anyone else could surely do the same." A pause, a measured inhale that spoke to simmering frustration, and at last Odona concluded, "If Baell would refuse to award a contract simply because I am unattached, imagine how she will react to infidelity."

And damn it, didn't Odona realize Addison had considered that? He had scoured local information for a spot to visit tonight—a place Baell's rich and pretentious family would avoid, but still safe and busy and respectable. It was unfair as hell for Odona to accuse him of endangering their shot at this job, as though Addison hadn't done his best to mitigate the risk.

He tried to calm himself, but the effort failed spectacularly. His heart had reached a frantic new rhythm, and his entire body ached for—

Something.

Fuck.

He was riled and energized, disappointed over the intimate companionship Odona had chased off. Never mind the risk of discovery—the chance of Anatoria Baell finding out—the logical arguments for stepping back and listening to what Odona was saying. None of that was enough to coax Addison away from the precipice he abruptly found himself standing before.

Odona had encroached into his space, and Addison found himself keenly aware of the thoughtless proximity. After all his years being *very conscious* that Odona was attractive—despite all the time he'd spent admiring without any particular urgency—why was this suddenly a problem? He'd never before found this man so utterly distracting.

Odona was the entire reason he'd come here tonight. If Addison didn't scratch this itch, he could all too easily picture himself behaving poorly. Saying something stupid. Giving away the fact that his view of his captain had taken a decidedly unprofessional turn.

The worst part was, he *wanted* to behave poorly. He wanted to so badly he could taste it beneath the more bitter flavor of frustration. He wanted to behave poorly *with Odona*, and this whole stupid field trip was pointless if he couldn't reroute his energies in other directions. The last thing he needed was the man himself barking orders at him, telling him he wasn't allowed to seek some other outlet when Addison already felt like he might explode.

So Addison ignored the apparent reasonableness of the argument and instead retorted, "You're being paranoid."

"I am being practical," Odona countered stiffly, clearly unswayed by Addison's blatant disrespect. "Your flirtations tonight are an unconscionable risk. What would you have done if someone from the compound saw you with that man? If they saw you doing... *that*, with some stranger, when you are supposed to be my mate?"

Addison blinked, parsing the words through. "Doing what? Kissing?"

Odona glared silently.

"You don't know what kissing is?" Addison pressed, not sure why it seemed so completely improbable. Hell, it shouldn't have been surprising. Kissing wasn't a Remian custom, after all. There was a reason Addison hadn't kissed Odona during any of their unscripted displays of public affection. And though Odona had intimated experience with previous lovers, their conversation last night hadn't gone *that* specific. Apparently this was one niche that had passed beneath his notice.

Except Odona was giving him an exasperated look now, a grimace with a hint of impatience. "I'm familiar with the practice."

Addison reevaluated. Odona was acquainted with kissing—recognized it for an intimate act—but the knowledge had clearly been gleaned at a distance. He didn't refer to it as though he had any idea what he was missing.

"Okay. You're familiar with it," Addison conceded. "But you haven't done it yourself."

The words were something of a gamble. It was entirely possible Odona had tried and disliked the experience. Kissing wasn't for everyone, and a personal dislike could explain the air of disapproval. But Addison didn't think any of that was the case. His gut said he'd found the more likely truth; and the way Odona's already confrontational posture went even more rigid at the observation... That was proof positive as far as Addison was concerned.

"I don't see what difference that makes," Odona protested, defensive but also soundly confirming Addison's thesis.

"I *like* kissing." Addison sat straighter and narrowed his eyes. "It's one of my favorite things about sex. And Bann was *really good at it*. He probably would have been good at other things too. You scared him off, and you *don't even know what you interrupted*." By the time he finished making his point, Addison's voice had devolved to a furious hiss. Better than shouting, though it was only Odona's nearness that meant the words were actually reaching him through the surrounding noise.

New tension wound visibly tighter in Odona's stance.

When Addison finally stopped speaking, Odona snapped, "Then why don't you enlighten me?"

The snarled retort halted them both, catching the air between them and twisting the whole of reality sideways. As the words hit home, the anger on Odona's face vanished instantly, replaced by an expression of guilty horror. It could not have been more obvious he hadn't meant to say such a thing, and in the black of his eyes Addison read a glimmer of desperation as Odona searched for a way to take the words back.

Fuck that. Odona didn't get to put that kind of offer on the table and then pretend he hadn't done it. If he wanted to sound the retreat now, he needed to own it.

Addison's voice smoothed—softer, like it was coming from somewhere completely different than the pit of riled confrontation in his chest—when he asked, "Would you like that, sir?"

"I didn't mean—" Odona started, fumbled. He looked on the verge of panic. But when he tried to take a backward step, Addison reached out and twisted both hands in the front of his shirt to stop him.

Addison gave a tug, and Odona stumbled forward, farther into Addison's space than before.

The barstool beneath him stood tall enough that the usual difference in their heights was minimized. Addison barely needed to tilt his head in order to maintain eye contact at close range. He found unexpected heat in Odona's startled gaze. And despite the threat of panic still obviously close at hand, Odona made no effort to escape again.

Addison felt a wicked smile creep across his face, and he shifted his grip. Gave a second tug that pulled Odona into the welcoming space between his knees.

This time Odona came smoothly forward, crowding Addison, leaning in with a look of warm disbelief. Odona bent one arm atop the table to Addison's left, bracing for... something. Addison didn't know either, really. What the hell was he doing? This was a terrible idea, but now he was here and he couldn't convince himself to *stop*.

"You okay?" He eased his grip from Odona's shirt, pressing his palms to the broad, deliciously imposing chest.

Instead of answering, Odona curled his free hand at Addison's hip and closed the last of the narrow distance between them.

And oh, yes, this was *definitely* a problem.

It was a cautious kiss. Odona's mouth was closed, his touch surprisingly gentle. Addison slid both his hands lower, slipped his arms around Odona's waist to tug him closer. Addison drew him forward until Odona was pressed intimately between Addison's thighs. Softness and sturdy muscle pressed against him, and the kindling eagerness in Addison's chest burned dangerously brighter.

He knew better than this. He knew damn well this was a terrible idea. But he wanted it anyway.

Addison broke from the kiss only long enough to murmur. "You can open your mouth. Let me in. I'll show you what to do." He sounded breathless to his own ears. Shaken and a little bit lost. The words stopped as the kiss resumed, studious but eager.

He nearly moaned aloud when Odona obeyed the quiet plea, lips parting like a question. Addison slipped his tongue forward, teasing and exploring. He was gratified—and aroused as hell—by the way Odona met him in this challenge too. Odona deepened the kiss with a curious slide of his own tongue, hesitation giving way to confidence with every passing second. Not quite taking command, but holding Addison tighter, pressing more forcefully against him as Odona took and took with increasing surety.

God, it felt so fucking good. Good enough that Addison broke away again and said, "You don't have to be so gentle."

Odona's hand disappeared from his hip and rose to tangle in his hair, and Addison gasped with pleasure at being dragged into another deep kiss. There was no longer any sign of the uncertain testing of waters. There was only the strength in Odona's hands, the slide of an arm around his waist, the delightfully filthy thrust of tongue past parted lips.

It figured Odona was a quick study. Fuck, how was Addison supposed to extricate himself and calmly return to the compound *now*?

For a final time they broke apart, both of them breathing hard. Addison's eyes were closed, and he kept them that way for a long time, even as he continued to hold Odona close—even as he savored the warm breath ghosting across his jaw—even as he willed away his body's predictable reactions to everything that had just passed between them.

When he blinked and actually *looked* at Odona, he didn't know how to read the glimmer in those impossibly dark eyes. Not anger, not disgust, not shame. Even if Addison feared those reactions, there was more tangible proof against them in the fact that Odona had yet to let go of him. But even without the worst contenders, there were still plenty of possible explanations for the wide-eyed way Odona was gawping at him.

Addison realized he was staring too. His heart beat painfully fast, and a threatening crest of panic twisted beneath his skin. A hot deluge of, *Oh fuck oh fuck oh fuck oh fuck* echoed alongside a repeating chorus of, *What have I done?*

More than anything, in that instant he wished he could parse Odona's expression. He usually knew with a quick glance what was going on in his captain's head, reading Odona with all the ease of their years in close proximity. Whether it was his own feelings clouding his judgment or some deliberate effort on Odona's part to conceal his reaction, Addison was at a complete loss this time. They stood together on uneven ground, and Addison couldn't breathe through the anxious whirlwind inside him.

Odona released him and took a single step back, forcing Addison to let go as well. The silence between them held taut and uncomfortable.

"Galin Odona?" a smooth voice interjected, jolting both men from their disbelieving stupor.

They turned their heads in unison, and Addison blinked at the woman who suddenly stood beside his table. Familiar. A guest from Baell's estate. It took him a moment to stop his senses spinning long enough to remember her name.

By the time he managed to extract the information from his reluctant brain, Mallita Denek was already speaking again. "I thought it was you. And hello... Addison, isn't it? Goodness, what an unlikely coincidence running into you two tonight, here of all places." Her tone—wry and thick as honey—made it clear this was no coincidence at all. Her expression was bland, but Addison still got the distinct impression she would pay good money to be anywhere but here.

"Good evening," Odona replied in an audibly strained voice.

"I don't blame you for needing a night to yourselves," she continued blithely. "I hope you're both having a good time. The estate is lovely, but it can be stifling." At least she didn't seem inclined to pretend she *wasn't* here as Baell's spy. The lack of explanation or pretext was refreshing, in a way. She must have tracked them down via comm link, the same way Odona had surely found him in the first place.

Mallita's gaze darted between them, willfully oblivious to the awkwardness of her interruption or the fact that she'd nearly given Addison a heart attack.

Maybe she genuinely hadn't seen them only a few short seconds ago. Maybe she simply didn't care. After all, even if she knew exactly what she'd interrupted, she had no way to realize it was out of the ordinary. They were supposed to be a mated pair. At liberty to touch each other whenever and however they pleased. They'd sold the fiction well so far, which meant she had no way to know just how unwelcome she was in this strange and tumultuous moment.

Then again, maybe it was a damn good thing she'd imposed herself. Addison's fight-or-flight instincts were rearing up something fierce. Given that there was nothing for him to fight, he was abruptly having difficulty holding his ground.

It occurred to him, fleeting and barely relevant now, that Mallita's presence proved Odona's point. Whatever the reason she was here, she knew them both. If Odona hadn't followed him tonight, Addison may well have been cozying up with Bann when she found him. A disastrous happenstance, especially since he was now certain she was gathering intelligence for Anatoria Baell. He'd seen the way she grilled Odona their first day on the estate; there'd been nothing idle in her line of questions.

"I—" Addison's mouth went dry, and it took him another attempt to speak. "I should go. I've got—Something. Something important to do. A communication to send." Smooth. Definitely not suspicious at all.

At least Mallita did not look offended as he slid down from his stool and eased away from the table. Curiosity glittered in her eyes, and she glanced back and forth between Addison and Odona.

"I hope you're not leaving because of me," she said in a voice that sounded almost conspiratorial, despite being pitched above the ambient noise of the club. "I didn't intend to interrupt your evening."

*Bullshit.*

"No." Addison sounded fractionally more steady now that he was actively retreating. "You've just reminded me of the time. But I'm sure I'll see you at breakfast tomorrow."

"Of course." Mallita nodded amiably

Addison turned away.

"I hope it wasn't something I said," he heard her say to Odona.

"He's just shy." Odona managed to sound only the slightest bit strained, even as he spoke the unconvincing explanation. Shy. As though she hadn't just caught them making out in the middle of a crowded club. "Let me buy you a drink. How are you enjoying—?"

Addison didn't hear the rest, and didn't care how strange it might look for Odona to stay while he ran from the club. He moved quickly now, making his escape up the stairs, through the enormous front doors, and out into the cool evening air. The dome above was dark, and hazy with a faint fog of clouds.

He drew a slow breath, filling his lungs and holding the air in for several seconds while he waited for his heartbeat to slow.

After a very brief eternity, he let the air out again in a steady stream.

He couldn't run away from this. Not really. There was no path forward that would allow him to avoid Odona completely—not without booking a ride off this moon and away from the *Korria* forever—and that was an extreme he had no intention of considering.

Which meant he had only one choice. He would return to the compound and wait. Apologize. Find a way to fix this. Find a way to stop wanting things he could not have.

In the morning they would finish what they'd come here for and put this disaster behind them one way or another.

# Chapter Twelve

If Mallita Denek found it strange that Galin loitered at the club instead of chasing after his supposed mate, she gave no indication. He didn't especially savor the idea of spending more time in her company, but buying her a drink—and then buying her a second one—was as good an excuse as any *not* to follow Valdez.

His reason, of course, was that he found himself completely terrified. He'd grown so accustomed, so capable, when it came to burying his feelings. He had mastered the art of not thinking about things he had no business wanting. But he couldn't explain away tonight's transgressions. Worse, he could only guess how transparent his show of jealousy must have been. Valdez knew him better than most. Knew his moods, his expressions, his tells.

Not to mention the physical intimacies that had followed.

The blatant invitation was no excuse: Valdez couldn't have expected Galin to call his bluff. And never mind the apparent eagerness with which every touch had been returned. Valdez would surely not have been receptive if he'd realized the true depth of feelings guiding Galin forward.

He was Valdez's captain. His employer. He had no business putting hands all over him—kissing him—

accepting an ill-considered challenge made in the heat of confrontation.

He had even less business wanting to do it again.

While Mallita didn't ask probing questions, there was something ferociously attentive in the way she watched him. An edge to her superficial conversation, as though she hoped for some sliver of gossip to report back to Baell. Galin had no intention of providing the satisfaction.

He did not offer to buy her a third drink.

"Goodness, it's later than I realized," she said before things could turn awkward. "I'm sorry to have taken so much of your evening. You must be anxious to get back to your charming mate."

"I hope you have a good night," Galin said, proud of himself for the way the words came out, friendly and almost natural.

"And you," she returned with a bright smile. Then she was gone, vanishing into the crowd so quickly Galin might have been offended under other circumstances.

How could he be offended though, when he was well past ready to depart this deafening club?

He didn't call a car, which meant it took nearly an hour to make the return trip via more public transportation. He navigated without difficulty the patchwork grid of hover lines and trains that ran only sporadically at this time of night.

By the time he stepped once more through the compound's main gates, he'd very nearly convinced himself Valdez wouldn't even be in their rooms. After the unanticipated intimacies between them, surely he would return to the *Korria* instead. For privacy and perhaps to air his grievances to his crew mates.

An uncomfortable thought, but one Galin could not shake and most definitely deserved.

He made it halfway through the main hall before Karnis Lor, of all people, materialized at his side. The hall was empty, late as the hour had grown. Despite the fact that it was the middle of the night, she was still dressed for the day. Karnis's crisp suit accentuated her narrow frame as she fell into step beside him.

"It's about time you got back. Anatoria wants to talk to you."

Galin stopped walking. "Now? Why?" It was far too late at night for business discussions, but he couldn't fathom any other reason for the summons.

Karnis only shrugged eloquently. "You think she told *me?*" Then, leaning close to murmur in a softer, more conspiratorial tone, "Between you and me? I think you've damn near won her over. Not that I doubted you, but... Well. Good job."

Galin didn't know how to respond to the praise, or to the hope dangling so temptingly before him. It was exactly what he'd wanted to hear since first setting foot on this estate, but he couldn't depend on it yet.

Not even coming from Karnis Lor, a trusted friend he had known for decades.

"You know," Karnis added, speaking at a normal volume again, this time throwing in a faintly teasing smile, "considering how often we've worked together, you could have told me *any time* that Addison Valdez was your mate. I've been treating him like a secretary for years. He probably thinks I'm an irredeemable snob."

"He doesn't." Galin's mind spun fast, conjuring details he hoped were plausible under the circumstances. "The last time I worked with you, we hadn't reached an understanding yet."

"Oh." Karnis nodded as though that made absolute sense. It should. Young as Addison was, Galin would hardly have looked at him as a potential mate when he first came aboard the *Korria*, and his professional partnerships with Karnis had always kept to sporadic endeavors. "Yes, I suppose I can see that. I'll try to stop kicking myself for missing something so obvious."

"Obvious?" Galin echoed.

"I didn't pay him much attention before," Karnis admitted, apparently oblivious to the audible trepidation in Galin's tone. She began walking, making a small gesture that indicated Galin should follow. She didn't continue speaking until he'd fallen into step alongside her. "I've been watching more closely since you both arrived. The way he looks at you... It's no wonder you couldn't resist the temptation."

Galin barely bit back the immediate question: *How does he look at me?* Asking such a thing would be damnably suspicious under the circumstances.

But he couldn't let the matter drop. He was too selfishly curious. The question he wanted to ask rearranged itself just enough in his head. A more casual tone, a hint of confidence he did not feel, a shift from disbelief to wry dismissal as he said, "I'm not sure what you mean. I've never noticed him looking at me any particular way." He kept his tone light. He needed to sound like a man with nothing to prove, to himself or anyone else.

Karnis laughed, dry but with a hint of affection. "Then you're not paying attention, my friend. The way he stares when he thinks no one is looking… It's charming, really. The devotion is there for anyone to see."

Galin breathed a noncommittal sound, even while his heart raced fast and frantic at the very idea.

It could not be true. Rationally he knew this. What Karnis took for devotion was nothing more nor less than Valdez's fierce attentiveness and unflinching loyalty. Given the farce they'd been playing out since arriving, it was no wonder Karnis had misunderstood. But that didn't mean any of this was real.

"I hadn't noticed," Galin said when the silenced stretched long enough to make it clear an answer was expected.

Karnis snorted. "How can you *not notice* such earnest attention?" Then, after a considering pause, she shook her head. "Never mind. I've known you too long to pretend I'm surprised. At least you noticed enough to do something about it. How long have you been together?"

"Less than a year," Galin said, despite the way his mouth had gone abruptly dry. "It's been... Unexpected." Plenty of truth here, at least. Everything about the past couple days had been a surprise. It would be a feat indeed to regain even a sliver of his former equilibrium.

"You're lucky." Karnis led him through a narrow door and into an automated lift that hummed to life and then hitched into motion. "Both of you. But especially after so long alone... I've worried about you, my friend. You never struck me as the type to spend your life partnerless. I'm glad to see you find someone who so obviously adores you."

It *could not be true*, Galin reminded himself viciously. Whatever care Valdez might have for him—and he was willing to concede there must be some—it was not the sort of regard Karnis was describing. How could it be?

And yet...

Galin had no explanation for what had transpired between them tonight, with no audience and no excuse to pretend. He certainly hadn't tracked Valdez down with any intention of stepping out of line, and

Valdez had clearly not begun the night considering such indiscretions—or at least, not intending to commit them with his captain.

And yet both of them had met there. Galin was far too accustomed to coveting Valdez to shrug off his own culpability, but he couldn't help wondering what *Valdez* had been thinking.

Before he could manage another coherent reply, the lift came to a stop and the door slid open. Galin followed Karnis into a hall significantly smaller than the one they'd traversed below. The narrower contours still reeked of wealth, from the thin blue carpet to the faintly shimmering patterns along the walls. Dimness indicated the late hour, but even this was eased by soft globes of bluish light hovering steadily near the ceiling.

Galin followed only a short distance along the corridor before Karnis stopped at a nondescript door. "This is it. I'm not invited to this meeting, so I'll say goodnight here."

"Thank you." Galin nodded. "Goodnight."

As Karnis moved unhurriedly away, Galin set thoughts of Valdez aside. He turned to the door—gray and wide and set deeply into the patterned wall—and touched the corner of the control panel in the frame.

The door opened with a sliding hiss, revealing a much more brightly lit office beyond. Galin stepped inside, seeking out and quickly finding his host behind the behemoth of a desk that filled one entire side of the enormous office. She stood between the desk and the massive window behind it. Her back was to the door, her arms crossed over her chest, her posture straight. The cane stood propped against the side of the desk, momentarily unneeded as Baell watched the nightscape city in the distance.

The office was impressive. High ceiling, wide floor, expensive art. It was just like the rest of Baell's estate, visibly careless of the fact that—in a domed city like this—every inch of real estate was invaluable.

Galin would consider it unnecessary, but such carelessness was its own demonstration of power. It made a statement to anyone who entered this room, whether or not they'd come to discuss business.

It certainly made an impression.

He stepped farther forward, and the door hissed shut behind him. He stopped a couple of paces in front of the desk, adopting a wide stance, clasping his hands behind his back. Waiting to be acknowledged. There was no official protocol for a meeting like this, but he followed his instincts and did not sit.

Baell didn't keep him waiting long. Good. Even if Galin had any extra influence to bring to this discussion, they were well beyond power plays and pretentious demonstrations. He and Valdez had either proven themselves or they hadn't. That Baell had summoned him tonight meant a decision at last, one way or the other. Surely there was no point keeping him in suspense.

Galin held his breath as Baell turned from the window and sat in the tall, plush chair.

"Thank you for coming." There was a wry edge to her voice. "I was beginning to wonder if I would see you at all tonight. When I sent Karnis to summon you after dinner, she informed me that you and your mate were both absent from the compound."

"I apologize for making you wait." Galin kept his tone bland, despite a burst of irritation. He could hardly be blamed for missing a meeting he'd never been told about. Beyond that, his private comm link had been active the entire time. There was no reason she couldn't have contacted him directly. Perhaps if she had, he would've avoided the new and troublesome tangle he found himself in with Addison Valdez.

He kept any hint of indignation buried beneath a more diplomatic front. If she chose to hold the delay against him, there was nothing he could do about it now.

"I'll skip the pointless digressions." Apparently she did not intend to offer him a seat, but that was fine. Galin remained standing, peering patiently down at her until she continued, "I've decided to award you the contract."

Galin allowed only a hint of the torrential relief to show on his face. "I'm honored to hear it."

"*Honored*," Baell scoffed, but not without humor. "After a thorough assessment of your character, I've concluded you can be trusted with the... *delicacy* of this assignment. I won't go into the details tonight. I'm sure Karnis apprised you thoroughly before dragging you across the sector, and the rest we can discuss when you review my terms."

"Speaking of the contract," Galin said, "when—?"

"Tomorrow," Baell interrupted with a dismissive wave of her hand. "I'll set my top legal advisers to draft the paperwork in the morning. You'll have whatever time you need to review the document before signing, of course."

"Thank you." Galin didn't know what else to say, or what else she might expect. If there were still details to negotiate, he would be far more certain what needed to be done. But it wasn't that kind of contract. Baell had not opened the door to discussion.

He was confident it would be a fair deal—Karnis Lor would not have called him in otherwise—but ultimately Baell had no obligation to negotiate. Galin would take or leave the contract essentially as written, and even that would be something of a farce, given the illegal nature of the services the *Korria* intended to provide. The true terms couldn't be included in the language of the document. This agreement was one of mutual trust, and if his gut had told him Baell couldn't be trusted, he would not be considering the proposal at all.

All this passed through his head in a whirlwind of seconds. The knowing way Baell watched him suggested she understood exactly what he was thinking.

Her expression could almost be mistaken for a smile when she said, "Get out of my office."

Galin ducked his head, not quite a bow, and said, "Of course. Thank you for your time."

## Chapter Thirteen

Addison had not stopped pacing in the deceptively short eternity since returning to the empty suite.

He'd paused briefly a couple of times, stood still beside a window or forced himself to sit. But every time he halted, he found himself up and moving within a few short minutes, too restless to remain motionless for long. Maybe he shouldn't have come back to the compound. What if Odona was deliberately avoiding him? What if he returned to the ship instead of coming here, and Addison waited all damn night only for him to never show up?

Odona would not depart Falaris without him—that much at least Addison was sure of—but as to the rest, he didn't know. He *couldn't* know.

Fuck, he'd kissed his captain. And now he had no idea what Odona was thinking or why he hadn't returned.

Predictably, the kiss kept replaying in his head. A perpetual and unproductive loop, vivid memory rising over and over again. It was distracting as hell, and it did nothing to quell his urge to panic. He had *kissed his captain*, and he cursed himself in the wake of his exceptionally poor judgment. Even though every measurable sign pointed to Odona having a good time, Addison could spot a bad idea in hindsight.

He also knew Odona well enough to recognize the utter shock that had preceded the kiss. Addison couldn't wave this off. He'd altered something fundamental between them tonight. Even if they returned to the *Korria* and never discussed it, they could never truly go back. Addison knew exactly what he was missing now, and Odona...

Surely Odona would never look at him the same way again.

At least he could console himself that Odona had been holding on just as eagerly as Addison. No matter how shocked, Odona had obviously been more interested than horrified. But that didn't mean he wanted this, especially considering he hadn't followed when Addison fled. Addison's guilty conscience gnawed at him with painful persistence. More than an hour since returning to their shared rooms, and Odona still *was not here*.

Maybe he wouldn't be back tonight at all.

Fuck, what if *Odona* felt guilty? There were plenty of practical reasons the kiss was a bad idea. Their working relationship featured heavily. Odona was his captain—his employer—and that complicated matters.

Odona wasn't the sort of man to put anyone in an uncomfortable position. No way in hell would he be the one to open negotiations. Even if he wanted to put his hands all over Addison tonight, he wouldn't say a word. Which meant any forward momentum would have to come from Addison, and even that was making the enormous assumption those advances would be welcome at all.

Well. Okay. Addison could work with this. He'd already dug himself into a pit of awkwardness. Might as well take things a little further; it would be immediately obvious if Odona wasn't on the same page.

He paced faster as he considered the possibilities.

There was something genuinely terrifying in the strength of the feelings igniting inside him, but he'd never in his life let fear stop him from going after a good thing. Why should he start now? Hell, even if it was *just sex*, that could be enough. Maybe all he needed was one chance to work this disastrous new infatuation out of his system. It would be a challenge, reassembling normalcy after a one-night stand with his captain, but at least he wouldn't spend the rest of his life wondering *what if.*

In the meantime, every passing moment left him more restless. He couldn't do a damn thing alone in this room. The confined space had grown stifling, despite how much larger it was than his own quarters aboard the *Korria.*

Approaching the two-hour mark, there was still no sign of Odona.

What if Addison had misgauged after all? What if Odona was horrified, maybe even angry? What if Addison had fucked things up so soundly they couldn't work together anymore? Odona wouldn't fire him—on that score he had complete confidence—but they'd spent years honing an efficient working relationship. They made a damn good team. What if Addison had managed to destroy that balance through his own stubborn inability to think things through?

Fuck. He was swinging back around to panic.

He forced himself to a standstill at the window and cast his gaze over the midnight-dark grounds. The lawn was lit in artful patches of subdued gold, and the buildings showed signs of life despite the late hour. Movement passed in occasional silhouette through brightly-lit windows in adjacent buildings. The sill was chilly beneath Addison's hands when he curled his fingers too tightly around the smooth edge.

It was almost impossible to stay put. Maybe he should take a long walk, somewhere he didn't continually have to reverse course upon reaching an unyielding wall. *Anywhere* beyond the confines of this private room. Damn it, he could wait all night only for Odona to not return, and what was he supposed to do then?

Addison let go of the sill and turned his back on the window. He'd kicked his socks and boots off the instant he entered the sitting room, the better to pace barefoot across soft carpet. He looked for them now, the first advance toward escape—

Before he succeeded, the hall door slid open and Odona strode through.

Without permission Addison's voice tumbled forward. "Where the hell have you been?"

Odona blinked at him for several seconds, wordless and inscrutable. The silence was enough to kindle fresh anxiety in Addison's chest. Odona was a quiet man, yes, but to see him genuinely lost for words was rare.

Rare and supremely unsettling.

Finally Odona spoke. "Baell is giving us the contract."

Oh.

*Oh.*

No wonder Odona was returning so late.

Addison took a step forward. "You met with her? Tonight?" Ridiculous questions. Of course Odona had met with her tonight. He wouldn't keep something like this to himself, and he wasn't a good enough liar regardless. The longer Addison *looked* at Odona, the more certain he grew that the dumbfounded widening of dark eyes had more to do with this new information than with the personal business that lingered unfinished between them.

"I did." Odona began peeling off his fitted jacket without moving any farther into the room. "She'll have the terms drawn up tomorrow. Then, with any luck at all, we should be able to make preparations for departure."

Addison still wore his own suit, though he'd undone the ridiculous row of tiny clasps along the front to let the jacket hang open. He was tired of stiff fabric and fancy attire. He wanted to return to the ship and his own wardrobe, his well-worn boots and comfortable shirts, his hair tied back without care for whether it looked fashionable. He wanted to be able to *breathe*. Fuck this estate and the people he was supposed to impress.

Odona folded his suit jacket over the nearest piece of furniture—one of the criminally uncomfortable settees—but he remained exactly where he was. At least he made for a nice view standing there in softer gray, thin fabric stretched over broad shoulders and the strong contours of his chest. Addison couldn't help looking and appreciating, but he did his best not to stare.

There was unmistakable reticence in Odona's stillness. Uncertainty in the perfect posture. Hesitation in the hands held behind his back.

There were wordless questions in the way his eyes followed Addison's every tiny movement.

Normally Addison could read Odona with incomparable ease—there was no one he knew better—but in this moment the ability eluded him. He knew what he *hoped* was going through Odona's head. But for once he didn't trust his own judgment. How could he rely on his own perceptions when wishful thinking might be clouding them?

Considering how powerfully he wanted Odona to touch him, how could he trust any of his senses to paint a clear picture?

He couldn't. That was the short and honest answer. He couldn't tell what Odona was thinking behind the intense wall of scrutiny. Odona sure as hell wasn't going to volunteer the information. Which meant they could spend all night circling each other in this useless standoff, waiting out a clock with no purpose.

Fuck that.

Addison wasn't a fan of stalemates, and he wasn't patient enough by half. He crossed the room with purpose and caution in equal measure, watchful for any hint of rejection.

Odona held perfectly still as Addison drew closer. No sign of retreat, no hint of rebuke. A glimmer of disbelief maybe; it was hard to tell when Odona's eyes were already so wide. But nothing to make Addison feel like his approach was unwelcome. He stopped close enough to touch but kept his hands to himself.

Peering up into Odona's face did nothing to help decipher the cryptic mix of emotions, but his heart pounded harder when his captain took half a step forward. The tentative movement put him directly in Addison's space. They still were not touching, but that hardly mattered.

Odona's willing proximity went a long way toward dispelling any lingering doubts, and Addison reminded himself to breathe.

# Chapter Fourteen

They stood quiet together for a long time, negotiating without words.

Galin's mind and heart were a chaos of feelings, all of them overwhelming, most of them contradictory. He wanted to take Valdez in his arms and never let go. He wanted just as desperately to run out the door—exile himself until this desire faded to something less urgent—something he could tuck back in the shadows where it belonged. He wanted to close the distance between them, but he simultaneously wanted to apologize and swear never to touch Valdez again.

Then Valdez set a hand low on Galin's chest—directly over his heart—and the deafening whirlwind of Galin's thoughts simply… Stopped. Replaced in an instant by a certainty he could not have explained if he tried.

The point of contact was almost too much. It seemed momentous, out of proportion to the simplicity of the gesture. Certainty twined even tighter beneath Galin's skin, warm and smooth and heavier every second. He moved cautiously, brushing his fingers over the Valdez's hand, deliberate and intimate, before covering it in a surer touch.

Valdez was cool—Humans ran physically colder than Remians—and he thrummed with discernible energy. Galin's heart pounded fast beneath Valdez's palm, speeding in the taut stillness. He wondered what Valdez's heart felt like right now. Probably a match for his own, considering the visible flush brightening his face. Such a torrent of unspoken feeling, when so far they were barely touching at all.

Then Galin raised his free hand and tucked a messy tumble of hair behind Valdez's ear.

The gesture inspired an instant reaction. Valdez pressed forward—up onto his toes—and took Galin's mouth in a pleading kiss.

Perhaps Galin should have hesitated. But for the first time he was sure of this, and he gave in to the heady mix of delight and relief. He twined his fingers in Valdez's hair, responding in kind. He didn't care about his own inexperience with this strangely satisfying Human custom. He might not know the first damn thing about kissing, but he knew the man beneath his hands. He knew this felt *good.* There was no point letting reticence interfere as he held on and accepted this wordless intimacy.

Whatever Valdez wanted of him tonight, whatever he asked for or offered, Galin was ready to listen.

When the kiss finally ended, Galin did not let go. He blinked, taking in the delight written across Valdez's face, the parted lips and closed eyes. His blood warmed at the low sound of pleasure that reached his ears.

"Valdez...?" he started, only for his voice to dissipate and leave him nothing to offer.

Belatedly, Valdez opened his eyes and peered up at him. "Addison," he corrected, and there was ferocity in every syllable.

"Addison," Galin echoed. He had said the name before, but it felt entirely different now. It felt like a privilege, and he liked it. Powerfully.

Another moment and Addison's mouth twisted into a wild grin. Nimble fingers slid up Galin's arms and grabbed hold of him. He startled when Addison began to back away, dragging him toward the open bedroom door. He managed not to stumble as he allowed himself to be led.

"This is all excellent," Addison said as momentum carried them across the threshold and over the narrow patch of floor, "but naked would be better." Even before he finished speaking the words, Addison untucked the shirt from Galin's pants. Cool fingers teased beneath the hem, seeking bare skin in brazen suggestion.

"You first." Galin's voice fell to gravel as he fumbled at the layers of *Addison's* clothing, impatience making him clumsy.

Addison shrugged out of his jacket, letting the sleeves peel back, and Galin took perverse pleasure in throwing the expensive garment to the floor. From the glint in Addison's eyes, he enjoyed the heavy thud of fabric too. A moment later and Galin dragged away the dark shirt beneath, an efficient effort with Addison raising his arms to help.

A pause then. An instant that stretched nearly an eternity. And then Galin dropped his hands to the fastening of Addison's pants.

"Can I?" he asked softly.

Addison froze so completely that for a moment Galin wondered if he'd gotten something wrong. Familiar Human eyes went startle-wide, and for several seconds neither man spoke. The interval stretched so taut Galin did not dare move, even to withdraw.

Then Addison blinked and his expression lightened. He raised one eyebrow, as though to dismiss the strangeness, and smiled a sheepish smile. "Of course you can. Did I say *half* naked?"

"No," Galin conceded. "You certainly did not."

He still maneuvered with caution as he divested Addison of his remaining clothes. Watchful for any signs of discomfort—any hint that he was taking things too far, too fast—but Addison only hurried him onward when Galin took too long.

There was sincerity in Addison's blunt impatience, and even more in the way he insisted on returning the favor. Galin raised his arms as Addison dragged the gray shirt over his head and then dropped it without ceremony to the floor.

He was only idly aware of Addison's roving, appreciative gaze in the moments that followed. How could he focus on *anything at all* beyond the vision before his own eyes? Addison stood completely bare, his compact frame practically vibrating with barely contained energy. So much naked skin, and after so long denying himself, Galin could not quite believe he was allowed to look. He was *welcome* to look. He could take his time and memorize every detail, every way in which gorgeous reality deviated from his own detailed and guilty fantasies.

For all the narrow lines of his body and short height, there was nothing delicate in the way Addison stood. Confidence kept his back straight, his stance determined. His hair was still down, the ends of those dark strands brushing bare shoulders.

Such an obvious and well-worn truth, but it still stunned Galin like a new revelation: Addison Valdez was beautiful.

He wasn't expecting to be pushed, but he let Addison nudge him backward, against the wall beside the door. He watched, confusion rising to match his arousal, as Addison dropped to his knees at Galin's feet.

"What are you doing?" He made no effort to mask his bafflement.

Warmth tinged Addison's smile, and his fingers slipped along the buttons of Galin's dress pants. "If you think kissing is fun, you're going to love the hell out of this." Then, expression sobering, he added more softly, "If you need me to stop, say so. Okay?"

Galin nodded, curious and a little bit stunned as his lust-hazed mind started assembling an idea of what Addison intended to do. He stared downward as Addison freed his cock from the confines of his clothing. The relief was so intense Galin honestly couldn't believe he hadn't noticed how uncomfortable the tight fabric had grown.

Addison was staring at his cock now, and the scrutiny made Galin flush with eager heat. Or maybe it was the curl of Addison's hand around him, the slide of a smooth palm, the swipe of a thumb through the slickness already gathering at the head.

Maybe it was the distracted way Addison's tongue snuck out to wet his lips as he gave a tentative stroke along Galin's entire aroused length. A second stroke ignited even greater pleasure, and then—shocking even though Galin had guessed it was coming—Addison's mouth opened and took him in.

The slide of wet, glorious heat was enough to overload Galin's senses, and he closed his eyes. His voice rasped a lengthy string of oaths, more profanities than he had uttered in the past several years combined. His head thudded heavily back against the wall, and he curled his hands into fists at his sides in order to stop himself from grabbing on with bruising strength.

Addison eased forward, taking more, and his hand slid away to curl at Galin's hip instead. Steadying and firm.

Lightning coursed along Galin's nerves at the hot, clever stroke of a tongue along the underside of his cock. He forced his eyes open—he needed to *see*—couldn't quite believe the input from the rest of his senses. But when he let his gaze track downward, the sight before him was even more overwhelming than before. Addison's eyes were closed, and he wore an expression of rapt focus. His dark hair was a staticky mess, his skin flushed as though with fever, and his mouth stretched wide around Galin's cock.

Somewhere in the last few seconds Galin had fallen silent. He could only stare now, winded and giddy and shivering from the mix of pleasure and longing twisted up inside him.

Addison blinked and strained to meet his eyes without pulling back, and they held like that for a long time. Several endless seconds of wordless understanding. Then, with a cautious touch, Addison took one of Galin's hands and coaxed it to relax, guided it to his head, and urged long fingers to thread through his hair.

The message was simple enough to decipher, even through wildly spinning perceptions. Galin tightened his hand where it followed the curve of Addison's skull. He held on with a teasing mix of command and tenderness, and Addison's audible hum of approval confirmed it was the right thing to do.

Galin's heart pounded faster.

"*Look at you,*" he murmured helplessly.

He was still struggling to draw a steady breath when Addison relaxed his throat and swallowed him down.

And oh—

*Oh—*

Galin's head fell back with a harder thump, and his cry of pleasure cut through the quiet room.

Despite the tidal wave of ecstasy, Galin made sure his grip loosened so that Addison could back off quickly. Even the retreat felt impossibly good, the slide of tongue and lips along his shaft as Addison held him more shallowly in his mouth. Galin didn't think he was imagining the glitter of mischief in Addison's shining eyes when he looked down once more.

He unclenched his other fist and touched Addison's face, brushing a thumb across the high cheekbone. "Do that again?" The words were a low, groaning plea.

The spark of heat in Addison's expression looked downright gleeful, and both his hands gripped Galin's hips tightly. When he pressed forward, there was barely any resistance at all—only the most fleeting sound that might have hinted at choking or difficulty—before Galin's straining arousal slipped smoothly down the back of Addison's throat.

Addison held this position for a handful of seconds before easing even farther forward—moving by slow, deliberate, maddening degrees. Galin kept his hand where it was, gentle but heavy. Patiently encouraging as he watched Addison's eyes fall closed, as he watched Addison take more and more.

The view was enthralling; he couldn't have looked away if he wanted to.

When Addison gagged around him, Galin relaxed his touch—gentling even more to make it clear Addison was welcome to retreat—but stubbornness predictably won out over physical discomfort. Addison refused to draw back, instead pushing forward. Swallowing more. Until his nose pressed to Galin's belly and Addison fell still.

The stillness was not perfect. Addison was shaking, both hands holding on so hard Galin suspected there would be bruises at both his hips come morning. Galin didn't mind the possibility, and there was pleasure in the faint discomfort. There was also no need to worry Addison might push himself too far. For all his fiercely Human determination, he also harbored better sense, and Galin trusted him to stop if he needed to.

He understood without any additional words why Addison had guided Galin's hand to touch him like this, and he barely hesitated now. He tightened his grip deliberately, an anchoring weight to keep Addison precisely where he was.

Even the faintest hint of resistance would break the illusion of force, because Galin would never hold Addison against his will. Any move to withdraw and his restraining touch would fall away in an instant. But he felt the brush of thumbs at his hips, an answer without words. Confirmation that they were understanding each other completely.

Addison finally withdrew, obviously reluctant about it, and Galin stroked his fingers through the soft, messy strands of his hair. Galin was shaking now too, inundated with sensation as his cock slipped past Addison's lips and into the open air. He watched Addison drag the back of a hand across his mouth to contend with the mess they'd already made. All the while Addison peered directly up at him, and the smile that emerged a moment later contained more than a hint of smugness.

Well. Addison had every right to be smug. Galin's head was still spinning from the pleasure offered by that talented mouth. Was this a Human custom, or something Addison had picked up elsewhere?

It didn't matter, really. Wherever it had come from, it felt damn good. Perhaps eventually Galin would get to make the attempt, though for now he was content to let Addison decide their course.

"Get the rest of those clothes off," Addison commanded, rising smoothly to his feet. "Then meet me on the bed."

Galin hurried to comply, moving with less than his usual coordination. Addison had turned his back— in search of something Galin could not guess—and Galin dragged his boots off, letting them thump to the floor. He peeled his pants away next, discarding every last scrap of restrictive fabric with a pulse of satisfaction. By the time he finished, Addison had apparently found what he was looking for: a small bottle that Addison removed from a pocket of abandoned clothing.

Discreet as the bottle looked, Galin still recognized it for the practical safety measure it was. Any irrational doubts he might have harbored about Addison's original plans for tonight evaporated in that moment. Edda Dak had most certainly *not* provided such supplies in their luggage, which meant Addison had made a detour to obtain it on his way to the spaceport.

Galin quashed an unwelcome pulse of jealousy and stood motionless near the foot of the bed.

Triumph glinted in Addison's face when he turned around, but he froze where he stood as though only now realizing Galin had followed his instructions almost to the letter. Wide eyes stared, triumph replaced with an expression of awe that swelled Galin's ego to ridiculous proportions. It was charming in a way, to be caught at the center of such riveted attention, and he did not protest the delay. He allowed Addison to look his fill, even as he savored the matching view. Anticipation sang along his skin, but he waited willingly.

Their vastly different statures posed a dramatic contrast like this, naked and in close proximity.

Galin's height and sturdiness made Addison's smaller frame look deceptively delicate alongside him. Where Galin was all broad muscle and imposing strength, Addison was narrow shoulders and lithe limbs, smooth skin that Galin knew he would be dreaming about for a very long time.

Tiny as the bedroom was, very little space separated them. Addison gave himself a visible shake and crossed the room quickly, reaching him in short strides.

Galin didn't know what to make of the seconds that stretched between them, or of the fact that Addison made no immediate move to touch him. Was he supposed to initiate? Did Addison expect him to reach out first? Perhaps he should ask. They had understood each other easily so far, but there were any number of ways they could still tangle themselves in knots.

Before Galin could reach any conclusions, Addison cracked a smile, wide but a little bit strained.

"I said to meet me *on* the bed, but I suppose this is close enough."

Galin's eyes narrowed, a fresh burst of caution holding him back. "Addison, are you sure—"

"Come on." Addison took his hand, interrupting with unassailable confidence. Urging him onto the bed.

They didn't bother tugging down the bedclothes as they climbed onto the mattress. Even the topmost blanket was unfathomably comfortable, and Galin was not inclined to care if they made a mess.

Addison moaned aloud at being pressed down onto his back and covered with the weight of Galin's body. The sound, helpless and sweet, sent a tremble along Galin's spine. The moan cut short with a kiss, and this too elicited warm shivers and a thrill of pleasure.

It had been a long time since Galin shared such intimacies with *anyone*. That it was Addison Valdez beneath him—a living embodiment of eager energy— made his pulse speed all the faster.

When the kiss ended, Addison gave him a dazed look before tearing his gaze away, suddenly searching.

Galin quickly figured out what he was looking for and collected the bottle Addison had dropped in their distraction. "Looking for this?" he teased. He bent one arm against the mattress beside Addison's head, bracing himself to keep a few inches of space between them. In his other hand he held the little bottle of slick. The smile on his face was fond and amused, and he made no effort at all to mask either feeling.

"Yeah." Addison swallowed, and his palms slid over Galin's chest. "You know what to do with it?"

A valid question. Galin had already proven unfamiliar with experiences Addison clearly considered commonplace. He'd never been intimate with a Human, and he had no way to know if Addison had bedded any Remian partners. He was damn sure *not* going to ask for such private details. But Galin knew what he was holding, and the body beneath him was similar enough to his own that he had every confidence they were understanding one another.

He breathed a soft chuckle and said, "Yes. I'm reasonably competent, despite evidence to the contrary." A more sober expression overtook him. "Which part do you prefer to—?"

"*Oh.*" The word was more needy gasp than conscious interruption. It was obvious, both from the helpless tone and the way it took him a moment to answer coherently. Even when he managed to continue, Addison's voice carried a breathless edge. "Oh, I *definitely* want you inside me tonight. If... I mean... Assuming that's what you want."

Galin considered the request. He considered the blunt sincerity of it—the clumsy honesty in Addison's choice of words—and the implication that they could change course if Galin had other preferences.

Another heartbeat and the smile on Galin's face spread so wide his face hurt.

"Yes," he said. "I'd like that."

He had made Addison set the pace getting them this far, but now Galin took the lead. He positioned Addison where he needed him, guided his legs apart, knelt in the space between. He nuzzled at Addison's throat, inhaling the scent of him as he snapped open the tiny bottle in his hand.

"If you need me to slow down..." He murmured the words against the underside of Addison's jaw, letting the statement trail off.

"I'll tell you." Addison's voice was thick with desire.

"Okay." Galin capped the bottle and nudged slick fingers into the space between shivering thighs. He found what he was look for—Addison't tight entrance—and traced a light touch along the rim, watching Addison's expressive face for any sign he was going about this wrong. When Galin pressed a single finger past tight muscle and into startling heat, Addison's spine arched and an eloquent gasp cut through the quiet.

Addison's head fell back against the pillow and his eyes closed, and for an instant Galin could not breathe. *Beautiful.* How could this possibly be real?

He shifted his weight and slid the touch deeper, unable to tear his gaze from the sight of Addison's face, gorgeous and slack with pleasure. It took several seconds for Addison to blink and meet Galin's stare, offering a glimpse of arousal and heavier feelings. The sight made Galin's chest ache, a sharp-edged and ragged yearning that he was painfully familiar with. He set it aside for later. Right now he had better things to focus on.

"More?" His voice rumbled with gravel.

"*Please, yes.*" Addison's answer was barely more than a groan.

Galin drew his hand back, then pressed in again, with two fingers this time. Stretching further, delighting at the slow but inevitable way Addison's body relaxed and adjusted. He thrust deeper, coaxing, curling his fingers. Loosening Addison by patient degrees. Satisfaction hummed through him when he hit a spot that made Addison cry out and clench both fists in the soft blankets. No hint of pain shadowed the sound; it was nothing but raw pleasure, fractured and overwhelmed.

"Oh *fuck*, do that again." Addison was breathing hard, panting and shaking as he spread his legs wider.

Galin happily obliged, memorizing every detail of Addison gasping beneath him, arching his back, writhing atop the sheets.

He lingered over his task, despite his own mounting need. By the time he withdrew his fingers, he had reduced Addison to a shaking, pleading mess begging for more. Addison's chest rose and fell hard with every panting breath, and there was impatience in the way he tried to follow Galin's fingers. Slick and loose, and obviously ready for something more substantial.

With his clean hand, Galin touched the side of Addison's face, carding long fingers through messy hair.

Raw electricity sparked between them when their gazes met. The exchange held an avalanche of unspoken meaning. Galin ached to continue, but he found himself frozen in this moment. Caught in a wordless acknowledgment of everything that had already passed between them, everything they were about to do. He was vividly aware of Addison's body, naked and cool against his own. Of glinting eyes and a winded expression. Of hands grasping his shoulders and Addison's mouth open as though in a silent gasp.

"Ready?" Galin asked, his voice thick with feeling.

"*God yes.*" Addison let go and braced his elbows beneath him, moving as though to roll over onto his stomach.

Instead of letting him reposition, Galin stopped him with a firm hand on his chest. He brushed his thumb back and forth over Addison's collarbone, a soothing touch. Pushed him down with gentle yet inexorable strength.

"Not like that," Galin said softly. "I prefer this way. On your back so I can see you."

Addison's eyes widened. Galin knew him well enough to recognize that there was a whirlwind of thoughts behind the astonishment, but for once he had no idea what the whirlwind meant.

"Are you all right?" He peered down into Addison's face, hesitating with concern. "If you don't want—"

"I do," Addison blurted. Another interruption in a long string of reassurances, as though he couldn't bear to hear the doubt in Galin's voice. Just like every other time, there was complete confidence in Addison's words. Whatever doubts had given him pause a moment ago, he must have resolved them almost instantly. There was no sign of reluctance now.

The stillness between them broke, and Addison arched against him. Galin fumbled with the bottle, then stroked generous slickness along his own length. Greedy hands found his shoulders again, slid over the muscles of his arms and held on. Galin pressed forward at the urging of those hands, letting his full weight bear Addison into the mattress.

Addison felt alarmingly perfect beneath him, taut and eager and sure.

Galin set the bottle aside and guided his cock between parted thighs.

He relished the tense instant before. The thrum of anticipation, the eagerness building at the base of his spine, the knowledge of just how good he was about to feel. He savored it now as he pressed forward, meeting lingering resistance despite how long he had spent preparing Addison. His heart pounded faster, and he peered into Addison's face. Hunger twisted hot inside him, but he could not afford to rush. He needed to make this good.

Addison's eyes were open, holding him in an unbreakable stare. Galin could not have looked away even if he wanted to.

"Do it," Addison pleaded. "*Do it.* Fuck me, stop dithering and—"

A forward stutter of hips, almost involuntary, and Galin gasped as Addison's body took him in. Addison swallowed a cry at the suddenness of it, but he also spread his legs wider, welcoming and wanton as Galin's cock nudged inside him by provocative degrees.

Galin stilled, then waited until he had Addison's full attention.

"I'm fine," Addison vowed before he could ask. "More than fine. Please don't stop."

Galin pressed forward, easing gradually but unrelentingly deeper. He moved slowly enough to give Addison's body a chance to adjust to the intrusion, but he did not tease. Now that they were here, he didn't hold back. And when Galin finally stopped, breathing hard, cock nestled as deep as it was possible to go, Addison gave a satisfied groan and dropped his head against the pillow.

"Still okay?" Galin settled more firmly over him, enjoying the way their bodies held perfectly flush. He nosed beneath Addison's jaw, gripped his hip with one steady hand.

Addison hummed an affirmative and twined an arm across Galin's shoulders. His free hand slid down Galin's arm, tracing bare skin and taut muscle. Galin's chest warmed at the obvious appreciation in the touch, and at the way Addison squirmed beneath him—not trying to get away—just finding the perfect position beneath the bulk holding him down.

"You can move," Addison said when Galin remained motionless. "You don't need to be gentle. I want to feel you. Not just now. I want to feel it later. Tomorrow. I want to know this was real."

Galin absorbed the admonition and rolled his hips back so that his cock dragged slickly inside Addison. Another moment and he thrust forward to fill him more roughly. The same sequence again a second later, but this time Galin thrust even harder, jostling Addison against the mattress. A third time, and the rhythm of it overtook them both. Addison arched and met each thrust, bending his knees and wrapping his legs around Galin's waist.

"*Fuck.*" Addison grunted when Galin upped the pace. "*Harder.* Fuck, I can take it, *please—*"

Galin had him pinned too tightly to maneuver, which meant he could easily ignore the plea. He could slow down, draw this out, make this last until Addison's begging turned incoherent, until they were both wild with desperation. There was nothing Addison could do to rush him without the leverage to force his hand.

But Galin's patience had long since dwindled, and instead he held on tighter and gave Addison exactly what he was pleading for.

He did not last long. The mounting heat coiled tighter and tighter inside him, culminating abruptly in a wave of pleasure. His orgasm was a noisy, messy chaos, cresting over his head and drowning any coherent thought. He stopped in that moment, motionless with Addison beneath him, his cock buried deep. He buried his face in the crook of Addison's shoulder, muffling his shout of satisfaction against sweat-slick sin.

It felt like an eternity before reality distilled around him once more. A shaky, endless moment passed as his senses calmed and his body quieted. Addison's hands continued to hold him, soft and soothing now. Stroking patient patterns into Galin's overheated skin as he eased down from the heights of his orgasm and finally withdrew.

Then Galin pushed up onto one arm.

"I've got you," he said, and reached his other hand between their bodies to grip Addison's cock.

He gave a firm stroke, circling the straining length with steady fingers. The sounds Addison made were the perfect guide for his efforts, as he repeated every touch that earned a whimper, a sob, a helpless moan. Galin worked with infinite focus, urging him relentlessly towards the edge.

There was no mistaking the moment Addison's orgasm overtook him. Expressive eyes fell shut, and he gave a wordless shout, twisting the bedclothes tighter in his fists. The slick release made a mess of Galin's fingers, but he kept stroking. More slowly now, a gentler touch, coaxing him through the torrent. Guiding him gradually down.

"*Oh*," Addison said, when their gazes caught and held in the stillness after. He looked dazed and, Galin thought, perhaps a little terrified.

Galin recognized this was no simple fear of *him*, or of the things they had just done. He knew Addison better than that.

If Addison was afraid, it was of unexpected feelings, not physical intimacy. A fact proven by the hand Addison set once more over Galin's heart, even as he stared up at his captain, stunned and helpless.

Galin couldn't blame him for being overcome. Four days had fundamentally shifted the very foundations of their relationship. None of this was truly new to Galin—he was well-accustomed to desiring Addison Valdez—but Addison? Addison clearly had not seen this coming. And perhaps when Galin had first returned to their shared rooms tonight, all Addison craved was a one-time encounter. A casual exchange to make up for the liaison Galin had interrupted at the club. Galin would certainly accept the unpleasant reality if this endeavor was not to be repeated.

But Addison's expression suggested more complicated feelings, and Galin's every instinct said this was something else. Something more. Something personal and intense, igniting a first glimmer of panic in the astonished Human.

Galin ducked his head before that panic could manifest, bestowing a chaste but lingering kiss.

Then he eased back, brushing sweat-damp hair away from Addison's forehead. He kept the touch gentle. Calming. When he shifted completely off of Addison and onto his side atop the mattress, he quickly tugged their bodies close once more.

He kept his arms loose, needing to be sure the embrace would be easy to wriggle out of if Addison did not want to stay.

"*Sleep.*" he brushed the word against Addison's temple. "It's late, and tomorrow could still be a very long day."

*

Considering Addison's habitual restlessness, Galin was impressed how quickly he stilled and settled. Easy to imagine the tumble of too many thoughts in his relentless mind, but those would wait. For morning, for clearer heads, for renewed energy to properly talk this through.

Galin still hadn't decided what to do about the lines they'd crossed by the time he realized Addison was already asleep.

Soundly, steadily, beautifully asleep. Addison's chest rose and fell in an even rhythm, lips barely parted. Eyes closed and expression slack.

Looking at him like this, Galin couldn't bear the idea of getting out of bed. He doubted Addison would wake, but that was only half the problem. The other half lay in the fact that in order to stand up, Galin would have to let go. Unthinkable in the face of the whirlwind of affection filling his chest—feelings he was allowing free rein for the very first time.

He was closer to the edge of the bed than Addison, so he shifted his weight. Rolled just enough onto his back to fumble for the nightstand, praying for— Yes, there, exactly what he needed. Nothing fancy. Just a discreet stash of tissues, certainly intended for less prurient uses. They did the job regardless, and when he tossed them to the floor—tomorrow's problem—he felt clean enough to sleep comfortably.

Addison was still out, and Galin smiled as he rolled onto his side once more, back into Addison's space. Every instinct said to crush him close, to hold on tight and never let go. But he was also painfully aware that one night of intimacy did not necessarily mean they'd reached any kind of understanding.

He *hoped.* He genuinely, fiercely hoped. He knew Addison well enough after years of watching him closely. For all Addison's impulsiveness, he was smart. Careful—almost methodical—when it came to important decisions and the people he cared about. Seven years ago, when he'd asked to remain part of the *Korria's* crew, he'd come prepared with a whole treatise of reasons he should be allowed to stay.

In the time since, he'd proven just as stubbornly thorough. Not always—certainly not when his pride or temper were piqued—but when it came to the questions that mattered most, he was unfailingly cautious.

*This* mattered. For Addison to want him was one thing. For him to channel that wanting into action— for him to *actively pursue*—for him to invite Galin to touch him... That was something more. He wouldn't deliberately confuse his captain like this. And surely he would not take such a gamble with their working relationship, if physical satisfaction were the only thing at stake.

Galin's confidence in this analysis didn't change the simple fact that they still needed to talk. He couldn't take his conclusions for granted, and he would not let assumptions lead to disastrous misunderstanding.

He intended to do this right.

Considering the messy chaos filling his head, he honestly didn't expect to sleep. But the day had been long, and his body was gloriously exhausted. He drifted off easily, into strange but pleasant dreams, full of warmth and unfamiliar roadways and expressive Human eyes.

*

He woke just as smoothly as he'd fallen asleep, to gray light through the window. Considering how early daylight arrived in this city, it must be barely morning at all. But Galin felt rested and luxuriously comfortable, and he stretched as his body acknowledged being awake.

Galin blinked upwards and found Addison sitting within easy reach beside him. Watching quietly, still naked as he sat cross-legged atop blankets they had never bothered to crawl beneath. Addison made for a charming image with the sex-and-sleep-wild tousle of his hair, and the faint blush barely visible in the tentative light. His expression was fiercely intent. He looked very much like he couldn't quite believe what they'd gotten up to last night.

"Good morning." Galin shifted on the mattress but didn't bother sitting up yet. He made no effort at all to mask the appreciative sweep of his gaze; if Addison minded, surely he would not be sitting so very close and so very naked.

"Good morning, sir."

The smile slipped from Galin's face. "You're allowed to use my name too, you know."

The faint blush burned brighter across Addison's skin and his eyes widened. "Fuck. Force of habit. I'm sorry."

"You don't need to apologize." After all, Galin's authority *did* complicate everything they'd done. He couldn't just ignore the fact that he was a captain and Addison his subordinate. A bossy, irreverent, argumentative subordinate who had no qualms about running Galin's business exactly how he pleased, but...

Still a subordinate.

To avoid acknowledging that underlying reality would be irresponsible. Everything they'd done—and that he very much wanted to do again—already crossed lines he had no business crossing. He couldn't very well be irritated with Addison for reminding him where they both stood.

He sat up slowly, barely resisting the urge to tug the bedsheets over himself as he moved. Addison's own nakedness seemed a pretty clear signal, but Galin needed to scout the terrain before he could be confident of his footing. He needed to be sure beyond any conceivable doubt that his attentions were welcome, and absent that certainty he would tread with caution.

When Galin was upright and leaning against the headboard, Addison's gaze swept down his bare chest, unmistakably appreciative. After a moment, that intense focus returned to his face.

A small but eloquent smile twitched wickedly at the corner of Addison's mouth. "Good morning, Galin."

Galin's own face stretched into a wide grin. The way Addison said his name sent pleasant shivers along his spine and made him ache to touch.

He sat still despite the renewed desire to reach out, taking in the sight before him with a watchful eye. He used every sliver of insight he'd earned over their years working together to try and decipher what was going on in Addison's head. Galin wondered how long Addison had been awake.

There, a glimpse and then gone, he saw the flicker of uncertainty in Addison's strange eyes. A glimmer of questions unasked. And he was almost certain he recognized the most urgent among them: *What happens now?*

"Are you all right?" Galin asked. The question was a gamble. He was all too familiar with Addison's prickly pride.

Addison's eyes narrowed. "Are *you?*"

Galin's smile softened—he couldn't help it—and he made no effort to contain the rush of fondness warming his expression. "To be entirely honest, I'm feeling a great deal better than 'all right' at the moment." The honesty was a gamble too, in its way, but he kept his tone light. If Addison made to retreat, Galin would not stop him.

But instead of retreating, Addison leaned fractionally closer. His face and chest flushed a brighter red. The intense gaze cut aside, evasive and self-conscious, but there was vulnerable candor in his voice a moment later.

"Yeah. Me too."

Every protective instinct in Galin's body ignited at the way Addison was looking fastidiously elsewhere. Taut potential coiled between them. They had barely scratched the surface last night, but Galin continued to hesitate. He felt increasingly confident he wasn't the only one who wanted more, but he was terrified just the same at the idea of overstepping. He could still conceivably be *wrong*.

"Come here?" he said finally, softly. Careful to make sure the words sounded like a question and not a demand.

Addison's attention snapped instantly back to his face. Another moment and Addison moved, rising onto his knees and crossing the bed with unexpected grace. Galin opened his arms. His head swam with a heady mix of relief and longing when Addison accepted the wordless invitation, crawling into his space and sitting astride his lap.

Cool hands settled on Galin's bare chest—a contrast to the hopeful inferno in Addison's expressive eyes. Galin's own hands dropped low, curling loosely over bony hips. There were bruises in the skin beneath his touch, a nearly perfect match, and Galin smiled at the memory of putting them there. Of Addison begging for more, harder, *please*, and the helpless sounds of pleasure when Galin gave him what he wanted.

Those sounds were a memory he would cherish forever, whether they reached an understanding this morning or not.

"You don't regret fucking me last night?" Addison asked, peering at him with unaccustomed ferocity.

Galin laughed, startled at the unlikely contradiction in the question. So blunt and direct, but with quiet uncertainty shivering beneath every syllable. It probably shouldn't have been nearly as charming as Galin found it.

He let mirth and affection shine in his face as the laughter faded. "Do I look like a man with regrets?"

"No." A second later Addison followed the concession with, "But for a terrible liar, you have an excellent poker face. Maybe you're just being kind."

Galin's brow furrowed. "I wouldn't mislead you." He set aside a faint pulse of hurt. Addison clearly didn't intend the words as an accusation. Galin knew what a poker face was—Addison had once insisted on teaching him how Humans gamble—but he also recognized that Addison wasn't truly suggesting this whole exchange might be some sort of elaborate bluff.

This was a search for reassurance; Galin was not the only one on unsteady ground.

"But—" Addison began, then cut himself abruptly short.

Galin considered taking his hands off of Addison, but couldn't find a way to do so without removing Addison from his lap. And while perhaps that would have been the smarter choice—perhaps it would make all of this easier to discuss with a clear head—he found the idea beyond his capacity.

"Please speak your mind," he said when it became evident the silence would continue. "If you're uncomfortable with any of this, I want to know. I *need to know.*"

Addison opened his mouth, but it took him a moment to speak. He was obviously collecting his thoughts, shoring himself up. The show of bravado lit a fresh ember of anxiety in Galin's chest. He began to wonder anew if he had miscalculated. Perhaps he'd been wrong after all.

But when Addison finally spoke, it was only to say, "You never wanted me before." There was something almost pleading in the words, and they made Galin's heart twinge sharply.

"That's not true." Simple honesty was the only path forward.

"It's not?"

Galin let out a slow breath. He'd come this far already, admitted this much, and Addison was still touching him. Feeling wild and reckless and a little guilty, he admitted, "I have wanted you very badly, for a very long time."

"You never said anything!"

Galin laughed at the outburst, the sound startling from him all the louder at just how *affronted* Addison sounded. "Of course I never said anything. I knew well enough that *you* did not want *me.*"

It was a truth he'd long since made his peace with, though it was only one reason he'd walled these feelings off where they could not affect his interactions with a member of his crew. Even if Addison had behaved differently—even if he'd flirted and teased and given any indication of interest—Galin would not have said a word. That they'd ended up in bed together was a lapse he couldn't account for, even as he acknowledged he didn't regret the path that had brought them here.

Addison licked his lips. "What about now?"

Galin huffed a short, quiet breath. "I don't think that's for only me to decide.

"That's the most evasive thing you've ever said to me."

A shimmer of amusement lightened the deluge of feeling in Galin's chest, and he shook his head. "It's not evasive. It's practical." When Addison only gave him a skeptical look, he continued. "I'm sure I don't need to point out that my behavior has been... less than professional. Or that the authority I wield remains a problem."

Addison blinked, and his mouth twisted down at one corner. "You haven't pressured me into anything. Your authority has *nothing to do with this.*"

"Addison please," Galin said softly. "I'm not denying you. I just need to be *sure.* You don't owe me anything. I won't be upset if you wish to put all this behind us and never discuss it again. And if you want to leave the ship, I know good people who could see you connected with a new position that is less... complicated."

Actual anger flashed in Addison's eyes, and he snarled, "Why the *fuck* would I want to leave the ship? Or pretend this never happened?"

"I'm not threatening to send you away," Galin murmured, aiming for the heart of Addison's protest. "I just need you to understand, you have options. Stay put or leave, pretend or don't. It's up to you. I won't put you in an untenable position."

Something new flashed in Addison's eyes now. Something almost hurt. A puzzle Galin could not decipher until Addison finally asked, "Are those my only choices? Leave or never acknowledge any of this again?"

Oh. Oh that was *not* what Galin intended. It sounded like an ultimatum when Addison phrased it that way. Stay or leave. No mention of how they might pursue this strange new connection between them.

Galin moved slowly, letting go of Addison's hips, taking one of Addison's perpetually cool hands between both of his own. His thumbs trailed over smooth skin and work-hardened calluses, and he dropped his gaze. Such an intimate touch, this steady press of hands. He wished it could convey his meaning without words, but he knew he needed to provide a more complete answer.

"For what it's worth," he said, raising his gaze once more to Addison's face, "I would be honored to call you my mate."

Addison inhaled sharply, but he didn't withdraw. A heartbeat passed, a sliver of tension, and then Addison's free hand dropped from Galin's chest and curled over the back of his wrist. A gesture of wordless encouragement.

"You don't have to decide right now," Galin pressed on before Addison could voice an answer. "If you don't want... Nothing has to change. Even if you stay. I want you to stay." Galin's heart beat faster as his confession settled between them. If they chose a forward path, *everything* would change. He could not keep sharing this intimacy with Addison and not ultimately need something more permanent.

"And if I do want things to change?" Addison leaned closer, bracing a hand once more on his chest, palm pressed to the spot where Galin's heart pounded a heavy, hopeful tempo.

"Then we will require a frank discussion of how to make this work and exactly what such an arrangement will entail."

"What if I already know what it entails?"

Galin blinked. "Surely you have questions."

"Fewer than you might think." Addison's confidence had apparently been restored, as a lighthearted smirk snuck across his face. The hand slid from Galin's chest to the line of his jaw, curling there, thumb brushing his cheek. "Gamina and Laia are surprisingly candid when it comes to questions about biology."

"Oh." Galin closed his eyes, momentarily mortified at the thought of his crew discussing him in such personal terms. Hypocritical, considering one of those crew members was currently naked in his bed, but his pride flinched just the same.

"I wasn't asking for sex advice," Addison quickly clarified. "I didn't— It wasn't about *us*. I just wanted to know why Baell was being such an asshole about you not having a mate. I didn't think about how it might make you uncomfortable."

Galin reopened his eyes. The worst of his existential discomfort was already fading, and he released the rest by conscious will. "It's all right. Better maybe, that you already know what the stakes are. Whether we marry or not, there will be... circumstances to consider."

"Circumstances," Addison echoed, and now he sounded almost teasing. "You mean your mating drive."

"Yes. That. And what follows. You know Remians mate for life. Exceptions are... not common."

"Of course I know." Addison sounded just defensive enough that Odona suspected this was a detail he had learned only recently. "And as for your mating drive? You'll have to tell me what to expect. But considering last night, I'll be looking forward to it immensely."

The words were light, but the meaning beneath them was so much more. It took Galin a moment to process the finality in what Addison had just proclaimed.

"Are you saying—?"

"I'm saying let's do this," Addison interrupted. He curled farther into Galin's space and ducked his head to nuzzle beneath his jaw. "And next time your mating drive comes, you take me and make it official."

"*Oh*," Galin breathed. Just the thought was enough to overwhelm his senses for several seconds. *Take me*, Addison had said. Like it was the easiest, most obvious thing in the world.

For several seconds perfect stillness held between them. Wordless longing twisted beneath Galin's skin, making it difficult to breathe. He'd been so thorough in pretending not to crave this, yet somehow here he was. Here *they* were. And he found it too improbable to believe.

"Are you sure this is what you want?" he asked, still hesitant. Still cautious.

"*Yes*." Addison's answer came out an exasperated growl. Fire flashed in his eyes when he twisted in Galin's hold, retreating only far enough to glare.

Galin tried to keep the answering grin from his face, but he couldn't quite manage the trick. He only smiled wider when Addison's brow creased.

Another moment and Addison surged forward, capturing his mouth in an eager kiss. Galin opened for him, letting his eyes drift shut. This was still such an unexpected bundle of sensations, Addison's tongue tracing his lower lip, and then a more deliberate thrust. It was remarkably reminiscent of other activities—a fact that could not be coincidence—but also strange in its own delightful way.

He could very much grow accustomed to this.

It occurred to him, only fleetingly, to wonder what time they would be expected for breakfast in the main hall.

Then Addison did something especially clever with his tongue, and Galin decided he did not care.

# Chapter Fifteen

They were, unsurprisingly, late to breakfast.

They arrived just in time to catch the final course, a strangely turquoise poached egg dish that Addison was far too distracted to properly enjoy. Despite the unbroken murmur of surrounding conversation, he found his attention slipping repeatedly—and predictably—to the man beside him.

It was embarrassing, really, to be so smitten he couldn't focus elsewhere. His senses had shifted. He was aware of Odona—of *Galin*—in so many new ways. Addison couldn't help remembering how those hands had felt, the slide of bare skin. His *mouth*. Who knew the man would develop such a quick talent for kissing?

Even better, Addison was allowed to want these things—he was almost certain to experience them again—and that was a heady thing to be certain of.

He liked it. He liked even more that Galin's attention kept drifting to *him*. There was no awkwardness when they caught each other looking. Only a flicker of heat, a faint exchange of smiles that went unremarked by their fellow guests.

There were less pleasant distractions to consider, like the fact that Addison genuinely had no idea what to expect of their final day at Baell's estate. Surely they had to wait, if not on the estate grounds at least here on Falaris, while her team drew up the necessary documentation. Even if the deal was for illegal services, he had no doubt the paperwork would be meticulous.

But how long would it take? What was expected of them in the meantime? How was he supposed to act in public now that he knew his captain vastly more intimately than he had yesterday?

At least the last was something of a trick question. They'd been pretending to be a mated pair for days; he could behave exactly the same. The only change was that the farce had ended. Galin was *actually his*.

Strange, how completely natural the knowledge felt. Considering all the things last night had upended, everything should have felt different. It didn't. Addison still knew his place in the universe, still knew exactly where he belonged. His whole world had tilted on its axis, but everything that mattered had stayed so much the same.

Galin vanished briefly as a final round of warm beverages was served. The hand that settled just for a moment on Addison's shoulder was a wordless admonition to stay put, so he did. He participated as much as he could tolerate in the surrounding conversation. Baell may have made her decision, but the contract and the cargo were not theirs yet. Addison could still find a way to fuck things up.

He startled when Galin touched his shoulder again a short time later.

"Sorry," Galin murmured on noticing his surprise, then gave a soft squeeze before letting go. "Let's return to the ship. I've sent our belongings on ahead, and Baell knows where to find us."

Addison was delighted to follow him away from the table. He waited until they were in an empty hallway before pitching his voice low to ask, "She doesn't care if we leave the estate? Without the contract signed?" He knew with complete confidence that Galin had not signed any documents without him; ever since Addison had taught himself the intricacies of interstellar contract law, Galin made sure to let him read every agreement before finalizing. A deal this delicate would be no exception.

"Baell will bring the contract to us." Galin's hand settled at the small of Addison's back, resting there with a new and familiar intimacy. "I imagine she will want to inspect our facilities. Besides, the sooner we're prepped to depart, the better."

Addison agreed enthusiastically with that sentiment. He was more than ready to put Falaris and the watchful eyes of Anatoria Baell's family behind him forever.

They borrowed transport from the estate—one last use of Baell's hospitality—and Addison felt an almost physical relief on stepping aboard the *Korria*, crossing the threshold of the ship he considered home. Galin wasn't touching him now, but it was obvious his captain felt the same. Addison could see it in the easing of tension through broad shoulders, the loosening of stiff posture, the not-quite-smile that softened the handsome lines of his face.

Home or not, there was no time to rest. Their crew mates were already busy; Galin must have signaled ahead to deliver the good news. The engine had been refueled, the manifolds calibrated, the nav console updated with the latest out-system charts. Edda was in the process of laying in their usual complement of supplies, which meant they would be ready for an especially long journey with as few layovers as possible. Plenty of other tasks remained, most of them dull, all of them necessary to a safe liftoff and voyage.

Baell arrived in the early afternoon, with three stiff- and official-looking employees in tow. They were unmistakably her legal team. All three hung back to the periphery of the common room as Baell strode forward and placed a delicate digital screen into Galin's hands.

Galin glanced at the screen, scrolled through the text. Then, without reading more closely, he handed the document to Addison. No instructions necessary: this was routine. Addison would be the one to read the contract in detail and look for trouble.

A quick scroll confirmed what Addison already suspected: the document would take time to parse.

Before he could say as much aloud, Galin slipped smoothly behind him and pressed a brief touch to the small of his back.

"Take your time," Galin murmured, then turned to Baell and her rigid entourage. "Why don't you all come sit down? Can I offer anyone a drink while we wait for Valdez to review the contract?"

"I'd prefer a tour of your ship," Baell countered. She sounded amiable despite her rejection of the *Korria's* hospitality. It was the more efficient choice, after all. This was almost certainly why she'd come in person rather than delegating or even digitally transmitting the proposed contract.

Galin gave a nod and ushered them from the room.

\*

In the subsequent silence, Addison put everything besides the contract out of his mind. He settled, alone, at the narrow table. He was confident Galin would keep Baell and company out of his hair as long as possible, guiding the guests through every corner of the ship. Addison preferred perfect silence for a task like this. He *could* focus under more challenging circumstances, but he did his best work in absolute quiet.

Despite the limited window of peace, he read slowly and deliberately. The document in his hands was a solid piece of legal construction, and a fair-minded agreement. It also did a remarkable job of sounding legal and enforceable, despite the nature of the service to be provided. The product was described in units, without any detail as to weight or size. Not entirely unusual, but certainly intentional given the nature of this particular arrangement.

Edda returned while Addison was reading the terms of compensation and final accounting. Gamina and Laia appeared soon after.

Addison greeted them all without looking up from his work, and they offered minimal distraction as they came and went and ultimately settled into the space around him. Edda sat at the table to his right. Laia took one of the couches at the opposite end of the room, with Gamina perched in her lap. Addison allowed the murmuring rise and fall of conversation to flow around him without breaking his attention from his task. The others talked about the job, the dockside preparations, the tour-in-progress they'd passed on their way through the ship.

Addison didn't mind. His task was nearly complete, and he had missed this.

His attention split more sharply when Galin and Baell returned, underlings in tow. The easy flow of his shipmates' conversation tapered off, replaced with pleasant but formal introductions. Gamina didn't bother moving from Laia's lap as everyone besides Addison exchanged greetings.

It was difficult to remain focused with Galin close by—a challenge Addison should have foreseen—but he kept his head down and finished reading as Baell sat in the chair across from him. Galin didn't sit, instead pacing the length of the room before coming to stand behind Addison. A moment, barely a pause at all, and then warm hands settled atop Addison's shoulders.

He didn't startle, though he caught raised eyebrows from Gamina and Laia as he set down the screen. He knew without having to turn and look at Galin that this was a calculated display of intimacy. A gesture intended to convey both affection and possessiveness, not for the benefit of the *Korria's* crew, but for Baell and her entourage.

"It's a fair contract," Addison said, making a point to look Baell directly in the eye.

"Of course it is," she scoffed. "What's the point of courting reliable talent if I can't convince them to stay in contact when the job is done?"

Addison cracked a smile. Galin's grip on his shoulders tightened approvingly, then vanished. Another moment and Galin claimed one of the few remaining chairs. He held out a hand, wordless and expectant, and Addison handed over the contract.

After everything they'd faced in order to win Baell's patronage, the actual signing of the agreement was underwhelming. Addison watched as Galin touched his palm to the screen to be scanned, and as Baell did the same.

"I'll have the shipment delivered by evening," Baell announced as she led her legal team toward the door, "along with a matching quantity of pigment modules for textile manufacture. Entirely legal for transport between the relevant quadrants. They should provide protection when you are inevitably intercepted and searched."

Addison blinked in surprise. He honestly hadn't anticipated such foresight. They could have—would have—easily obtained such a pretext before crossing sectors. For Baell to simply *provide them* with such a safeguard... It wasn't without precedent, but he certainly hadn't expected it.

"Thank you," Galin said, in a tone that made it clear he was just as pleasantly surprised.

Baell turned in the open doorframe and offered a wry look that could almost be mistaken for a smile. "I don't care what you do with the modules, so long as you make an effort to get *something*. Sell them for the best price you can get once the real merchandise is dealt with. You can account the additional profits when we negotiate our next venture."

Addison bit the inside of his cheek to keep from grinning at the implication: that this was only the first job of many. Maybe she would consider contracting them for legitimate work. Even if she didn't, this was sure to be a lucrative relationship for both parties.

"I'll escort you back to the main port terminal." Galin rose now, belatedly, and moved to join her at the door.

"Thank you, Captain."

Immediate silence descended with guests and captain gone. Even with his eyes turned on the empty doorway, Addison could feel his friends watching him with unvarnished curiosity. Thankfully, they were too cautious to ask uncomfortable questions about the past few days while Baell was still onboard.

Addison didn't acknowledge the attention. Hell, he didn't even turn to look at them before darting through the door himself, into the ship's central corridor. Not to follow, but to make himself busy— hopefully busy enough to avoid an interrogation about his epic misstep and his days pretending to be Galin's mate. There was never any shortage of tasks on a spaceship, especially one about to depart for a lengthy trip. As long as he kept moving, he could dodge any prying curiosities.

He succeeded so well that the next face he saw— three hours later—was Galin's. Far too long for a simple trip to the terminal and back, which meant he had managed other business while he was out. Departure permissions and customs forms, probably. For all the technology available at a top-of-the-line port like Falaris, some things were still easier to do in person.

"Our cargo will arrive dockside within two hours." Galin spoke the words quietly, appearing abruptly at Addison's side.

Addison lowered the safety checklist he'd been reviewing, resting his arms atop the high guardrail that protected this walkway from a nasty fall to the cargo bay floor. Even when he turned to face Galin more directly he had to tilt his head back. He didn't mind; he *liked* having Galin this close. Seemed almost too good to believe, that this was the new baseline for normal.

"We've set up a partition to keep the true cargo out of sight," Addison reported. "The fake bulkhead is astonishingly convincing."

The bulkhead was Gamina's work. They'd managed a similar trick before, but never to conceal so large a portion of the cargo bay. It was impressive, both in the skill of the illusion and the speed with which she'd pulled it off.

Galin nodded and cast a brief glance across the open space, currently empty. "I thought the hold looked smaller. Are we ready to accept delivery?"

"Yes. And ready to leave as soon as we do, assuming you got us cleared. Edda's finished stowing our supplies. Gamina and Laia have the engines fueled and primed. We can lift off the second we have the cargo secure."

"Good." Galin turned to regard Addison once more, warmth glinting in the black of his eyes, a hint of smile at one corner of his mouth. "Are we alone?"

Addison's heart pounded faster. "Edda's in the galley, Laia's doing preflight safety checks in the cockpit, and you know how Gamina is. She won't come out of the engine room until we break from orbit."

The hint of smile brightened and spread wider. Galin plucked the data screen from Addison's hands, shutting it down and compressing it. In its smaller size, the screen fit easily in the pocket of Addison's jacket—not the stiff-collared fancy attire he'd been wearing for the past four days, but his jacket—and Galin slipped the device away so deftly Addison barely felt the touch.

All of this was too blatant an invitation to resist, and Addison pressed forward onto his toes. Galin was still too tall to reach, but that didn't matter when they met halfway. Galin tilted his head down to meet him, pulling him close and accepting the kiss with enthusiasm. Only a handful of hours had passed since they were last alone, but it felt like an eternity when all Addison wanted was *more*.

He breathed a shameless, needy sound when the kiss ended too soon, not the slightest bit pacified by the affectionate graze of lips at his temple. Galin's chuckle lingered in the high-ceilinged hold, and his arms remained where they belonged around Addison's waist.

"Why are you stopping?" Addison stretched up to nuzzle beneath his jaw.

Galin breathed an exasperated sound but still did not let go. "Because much as I would love to debauch you, this is neither the time nor the place for such indulgence."

And oh, that wasn't fair. Who the hell did Galin think he was, throwing around words like *debauch* and *indulgence* while simultaneously threatening to exercise enough self-control for both of them? Addison relished the warmth along his front, the strength in the arms holding him. He wanted to continue this. He wanted it so badly his mouth was already watering.

"We could retire to your quarters." It would solve the problem of location at least. Surely that counted for something.

Galin laughed again, louder this time, and drew back to meet Addison's pleading eyes. "No, we could not. Not if we want to depart on schedule. Baell's delivery will arrive at any moment, and there's too much to finish in the meantime."

"But—"

"Soon," Galin interrupted gently. When his embrace loosened and he took a step back, every movement conveyed reluctance to put any distance between them. A moment later and he reached for

Addison's hand, drawing it toward him and letting his fingers trace the soft skin of Addison's palm. A lover's touch. A promise, in its own way. "Once we're en route, we will have ample time for such diversions."

Addison schooled his expression into a glare, but he made no move to withdraw his hand. "I'm holding you to that, old man."

Then Galin was gone, as suddenly as he'd appeared in the first place—vanishing deeper into the ship and leaving Addison to his work.

He finished quickly in the cargo bay, and with no immediate urgent task calling to him after, he made his way out of the hold. There was no one in the common room or in the galley when he ducked inside in search of water. The glass was chilly in his hands, and he settled at the common room table, surprised at how tired he suddenly felt. Less the fatigue of hard work than the result of too little sleep the night before, but Addison regretted nothing.

The glass was almost empty in his hands when Edda stepped into the room.

Edda took one look at him and announced, "You look tired as hell. I'm making coffee."

"Bless you and your entire family," Addison said. Coffee was an excellent idea. He should have started a pot brewing himself. Now that his more basic thirst was satisfied, coffee sounded like absolute heaven. He fetched more water anyway as Edda puttered with the

YOLANDE KLEINN

not-at-all standard apparatus the *Korria* used for brewing hot beverages of every kind.

"You know Anatoria Baell is long gone, right?" Edda said as he worked. "Her business here is done; she won't be coming back to the ship."

Addison blinked at Edda's back. "Of course I know that. She was only here to inspect the vessel and sign the contract."

"Right," Edda agreed, finishing his work and turning to face Addison directly. He crossed his arms over his chest and stared as though Addison was missing something obvious. "So you and the captain don't have to put on a show anymore."

Addison stared, caught-out and startled. He could feel his eyes flashing too wide, his face heating, his pulse rushing as he realized Edda must have seen them in the cargo bay and assumed... What? That they were still maintaining the illusion?

"Gamina told me what happened at Baell's estate. I wish I could've been there to see it and laugh at you, but you don't need to *keep* pretending to be Odona's mate. This isn't—" Edda stopped abruptly, a protracted pause as the information realigned in his brain. "Wait. You knew she was gone."

Fuck, Addison needed to speak. He needed to answer, deflect, change the subject. Rationally he knew—had known from the moment he set foot aboard the *Korria* this morning—that there would be no keeping this secret. Not in the longterm. Not on a tiny ship with all of five people onboard, and certainly not when his crew mates knew him so well.

But he'd hoped for a little time to catch his balance first.

"Edda—" he started, at a loss but needing to say *something.*

"Oh hell," Edda interrupted, smooth and high and disbelieving. "You didn't."

Addison froze for only a heartbeat, but it was still too long. He saw comprehension break crystal clear across Edda's face, dark eyes flashing impossibly wide.

"You did!" Edda uncrossed his arms and burst forward a helpless step. "You and the captain. When— How long have you— Are you *kidding me* right now?"

At least, for all the shock sharpening Edda's voice, there was no hint of anger. No suggestion that he was upset beneath his surprise. Dubious at being misled, maybe, but there wasn't much Addison could do about that. After all, he and Galin had only been keeping this secret for a day.

Not even a day. God, Addison had never been quite this terrible at secrets before.

"Gamina said it was just an act," Edda protested more calmly.

"It was." Addison sounded defensive even to his own ears.

"But it's not anymore," Edda concluded. An instant of total stillness held him, and then he turned for the door, abandoning the still-brewing coffee.

Addison didn't even have a chance to ask where he was going before Edda vanished through the open door already shouting. "*Gamina! Laia! Whatever you're working on, put it down. You are not going to believe this!*"

For several seconds Addison simply stared at the empty door frame.

He wasn't sure what to do. Even if it weren't already too late, there was no point trying to convince Edda to keep quiet. He had no reason to guard a secret so temporary. The crew would've noticed immediately when Addison moved into Galin's quarters—a detail he and Galin hadn't yet discussed, but it seemed inevitable—not to mention the newfound intimacy settling more solidly between them every moment.

Well. Maybe it was simpler this way. He didn't need to figure out how to broach the subject if everyone already knew.

He rose to his feet. Assuming Galin wasn't *with* Gamina or Laia right now, Addison needed to warn him. Their secret was out.

And Addison found—surprising but decisive—he did not mind one bit.

*Epilogue*

They spent a month in transit, careful and steady and garnering as little attention as possible. The stops they put in along the way were brief and efficient—refuel, restock, depart within hours—and no one paid them any mind. It helped that they'd run similar routes delivering legitimate merchandise. They weren't complete strangers in most of these ports.

Galin had cultivated a reputation over his years in the freighting business, and his standing served him well now.

There were no close calls, no narrow escapes, no run-ins with authorities too interested in their business. Galin would not breathe easy until their cargo was unloaded and far behind them, but he couldn't dismiss their good fortune in the journey.

Of course, his professional endeavors were not all he had to contend with.

It came over him so gradually he didn't realize for two full days. It might have been longer; he couldn't be completely sure *when* it first started. It only became obvious once he recognized the itch under his skin for exactly what it was.

Only four months had passed since the last time his mating drive snuck up on him. An unlikely interval, but Galin harbored no confusion as to why.

At least circumstances were different now. For once he had nothing to hide.

It was still not ideal. He was in the middle of a job—a period not at all convenient for personal considerations. One month since departing Falaris with their cargo, and the *Korria* was less than a day from its destination. Galin had arrangements to make, preparations to lay in, discreet communiqués to exchange. There was plenty of work to be done; he couldn't afford to barricade himself in his quarters with Addison the way the burning possessiveness in his blood urged.

He nearly did anyway. Addison, always close at hand and far too attentive, was even more so since their new understanding. No hesitation, no change of heart. After weeks of newfound closeness, Addison seemed every day more determined to burrow deeper into Galin's life and heart.

This inclination was one Galin vehemently shared. And now, caught off guard yet unsurprised that his mating drive had come upon him, all he wanted was to get Addison alone and thoroughly claim him.

He resisted. Galin was captain of this ship. The *Korria's* crew was tiny, and they each had their own duties, responsibilities, obligations. He could not simply take a day off just as his crew approached completion of their contract.

He'd survived inconvenient timing before. He would survive this. Quietly. Calmly. Just as he always did. And if it passed before they managed to complete their transaction, so be it. Next time he would be ready to do this right.

That was his plan. It was a *good* plan. Solid and workable, if far from ideal.

But it was also a plan that did not take Addison Valdez into account.

"You've been hiding from me all morning." Addison's voice broke across his distraction like a signal flare, and Galin glanced up from the documents displayed across his desk.

He hadn't noticed the quiet slide of his office door, or the footsteps of someone stepping across the threshold. Yet there Addison stood, just inside the open doorframe. His feet were planted in a stubborn stance, his arms crossed over his chest. Addison glowered across the small room with an air of disapproval.

"I am not hiding," Galin protested, shoulders tensing as every sense registered Addison's coveted presence. "I am *working.*"

Addison touched the faintly glowing control panel beside the door, closing them in and locking the office. A very few steps brought him to stand immediately in front of Galin's desk. He glared down, but up close it was easier to see the nuance beneath the expression. Exasperation and affection warred alongside stern annoyance. Galin knew full well that Addison did not like to be ignored.

"Are you going to tell me what's bothering you?" Addison leaned forward and pressed his palms flat to the surface of the desk, heedless of the display panels he covered in the process. The movement brought him maddeningly near and made it difficult for Galin to stay sitting behind the desk.

"Yes," Galin said in a tight voice. "*After* we reach our destination and complete delivery."

"That's hours from now."

"It will have to be soon enough." Galin forced his eyes back down to his desk and the unobscured data screen between Addison's hands. He kept his gaze turned downward as Addison straightened and circled the desk. Refused to look up even when Addison perched on the edge of the smooth surface, close enough to touch.

"You know I'm *right here*," Addison said softly. Knowingly. He had obviously sussed out the source of Galin's restless mood. "There's no reason to torture yourself."

"We can talk about this later."

"Or..." Addison reached down to curl steady fingers beneath Galin's chin, guiding his head up so that he could not avoid meeting Addison's eyes. "We can talk about this now. It's your mating drive, isn't it? That's why you've been on edge."

"Yes." There was no point lying. This wasn't some ugly secret. It wasn't a secret at all anymore.

"Then put the damn reports away and *fuck me*."

The way he spoke those words ignited a fresh blaze of desire beneath Galin's skin. Addison managed to sound so direct and easy and exasperated all at once. Galin already craved him with a potency he could barely ignore. Now, with Addison's blunt invitation echoing in his ears, he needed to close his eyes and breathe deeply just to maintain his composure.

"I have work to do." Galin opened his eyes. "We *both* have work to do."

"Work you can barely focus on!" Addison glared harder. "This is ridiculous. I know you haven't changed your mind about me, so why are you being such a martyr?"

"We will be docking in a *matter of hours*," Galin snapped, desperate in the face of fraying willpower. What Addison was proposing... It would not be a brief encounter. Desperate as Galin was to drag him back to their bed and accept the sincere offer, he couldn't. Not yet. Not when doing so would mean shirking final preparations and potentially missing the moment of delivery entirely.

"So?" Addison countered, smooth and careless.

Galin's eyes narrowed and his heart beat faster, a quick rhythm low in his chest. "So you know full well that once we begin I will not be inclined to pause our... interlude for the sake of business." Even now the thought of allowing Addison to leave this office was almost physically painful. To touch him and then let go before his biology finished running its course... The thought was not a pleasant one. "I cannot be *locked in my quarters* when it's time to deliver on our most important contract in months. My needs will have to wait."

"Fuck that." Addison hopped down from his perch, landing gracefully and turning around to activate the comm panel at the edge of the desk. "Laia, how would you feel about handling the cargo prep and delivery, so I can put the captain under house arrest until tomorrow?"

"*Addison*," Galin protested, straightening in his chair and trying to reach the panel only to be swatted away. It was too late, in any case. The question had been given voice; there was no taking it back. Even worse, Addison was blocking him from the controls, keeping his body in the way. If Galin wanted to close the comm line now, he would have to bodily remove Addison from behind the desk—and that much physical contact would make this losing battle all the more hopeless.

Laia's answer came almost instantly, carrying audible relief. "Yes. Terrific. *Absolutely.* Just keep him out of the cargo bay and we'll handle everything."

Galin subsided and stared past Addison at his desk, even though there was no image to go with the voice. He felt oddly offended, as though the comm panel had personally betrayed him.

Perhaps it was a sign of just how far out of control he'd spun that without a thought he blurted, "I haven't been that bad. Have I?"

There was a wry snort and then Gamina's voice, slightly more distant, cut into the conversation. "You've been worse. Do us all a favor and go away. We can handle things without you."

"Thanks, guys." Addison shut down the line and turned around, and there was no mistaking the smugness written across his face.

"I should dock your pay," Galin muttered. "Insubordination. Undermining my authority. This is mutiny, you know." He didn't mean it. Any of it. His crew had always harbored an irreverent attitude toward the chain of command, and even if they hadn't, Addison was *right*. And though Galin felt guilty at the thought of leaving his work on someone else's already busy shoulders, he couldn't deny the relief already coursing through him.

Or the urge to put his hands on the beautiful young man smirking at him.

"You'll do no such thing," Addison countered, though another moment and the smugness faded from his expression. He spoke more quietly, a serious undertone to the words. "Look, if there's some other reason you don't want to do this right now, *tell me*. I'm not trying to corner you here. I just want to help."

Galin's blood warmed, fondness twisting in his chest, and he stood from his chair. The change in position put him directly in Addison's personal space and emphasized the disparity in their statures. "Help?" he echoed teasingly. "Is that all?"

"Of course that's not all." Addison leaned back against the edge of the desk and tilted his head to maintain eye contact. Nimble hands twisted in the front of Galin's shirt. "I can be selfish at the same time. So stop being a tease and *take me to bed.*"

Galin shivered with pleasure and leaned in closer. He touched Addison's face, tracing his fingers along Addison's temple, cheekbone, jaw. He savored the flash of heat in expressive eyes. Most days he was still in awe that this clever, ambitious, utterly distracting Human was his. It didn't seem possible.

Perhaps that was why Galin asked, "Are you sure this is what you want?"

Addison had been sharing his bed for weeks, but this was different. This made it real, and the last thing he wanted was to trap Addison at his side if there were any lingering doubts.

Silence closed in around them, but it was a soft sort of quiet. The expression on Addison's face shone bright with feeling as he reached up to take Galin's hand—as he traced a touch like a promise along Galin's fingers. Addison's hand was trembling just a little.

Or perhaps it was Galin who couldn't quite keep steady.

"Of course I want this." Addison's gaze held unbreakable, and he sounded equal parts ferocious and exasperated. "I *love you*, Galin. And I'm not going anywhere. You can stop trying to talk me out of a good thing."

"Addison—"

"I'm already yours, okay? And I'm pretty sure you're mine. So let's make this official." Then, with just a hint of mischief, Addison tugged him down into a kiss.

New warmth ignited between them, and Galin slipped his arms around Addison, all the better to tuck him close and hold on. It was a good kiss. Eager with wordless suggestions, and promise, and more than a hint of impatience.

Galin had very much come to enjoy the nuances of kissing. He wondered how he'd ever managed without this. He wondered, with even more intensity, how he had ever lived without Addison Valdez.

He breathed a protesting sound when the kiss broke, but Addison only grinned and twisted out of his arms.

"Come on, old man. Race you to your quarters."

Then Addison was gone, out the door in a graceful rush, and Galin followed close behind.

*The End*

## About the Author

Yolande Kleinn may be a shameless dreamer and a stubborn optimist, but she is also a proud purveyor of romance and erotica. Excitable, fastidious and a little eclectic, she spends every spare moment writing the stories she wants to read. If she can drag other people into the pool along with her, then so much the better.

You can find Yolande via her website:
yolandekleinn.com

ASHES ON A DISTANT WIND

Before the Vrete came to Earth, Donovan Riggs was a man of faith. Now they're gone, and he's left that part of himself behind for good. In the ruinous aftermath of a war nobody won, he is simply trying to survive. With Beau Greer—a young medic who stumbled into his life and then refused to leave—Riggs travels dangerous roads between long-dead cities. Scavenging doesn't offer much of a future. It barely provides for the present. But Riggs will do anything to protect what's his.

EVERY SECOND YOU'RE ALIVE

Major Franklin Cade has spent years fighting the undead scourge that drove humanity from Earth. Now victory is in sight, but it's come at immeasurable cost. He has sacrificed everything in the line of duty—even his own heart.

For six months Lieutenant Daniel Mendoza has been missing in action. Only stubbornness and a refusal to tarnish Mendoza's memory have kept Franklin alive since losing the man he wouldn't admit he loved.

When a perilous rescue needs volunteers, he returns

to the canyon where Mendoza fell. He is not prepared for the hope that ignites as he follows a fading distress signal across infested terrain. In the shadow of a deadly countdown every second is precious, but Franklin refuses to lose Mendoza again.

## OPEN SKIES

After seven years working as partners, Kai and Ilsa are the best professional finders in the business. There's nothing they can't track down, no matter how unfamiliar the star system or hazardous the path. When a new client insists on accompanying the search for his daughter, Ilsa and Kai reluctantly agree. How can they refuse when Eleazar Dantes is desperate enough to pay double their usual fee?

But a high-stakes investigation is no time for distractions. Even more troublesome, when Kai realizes his true feelings for Ilsa, his timing couldn't be worse. Never mind that she doesn't seem to reciprocate: heartbreak is the least of their problems as the trail they're following grows dangerous.

With every step forward, Kai and Ilsa are more certain they won't find Eleazar's missing daughter alive.